Rumi and the *Red Handbag*

Rumi and the *Red Handbag*

a novel by

SHAWNA LEMAY

Palimpsest Press
1171 Eastlawn Ave.
Windsor, Ontario. N8S 3J1
www.palimpsestpress.ca

Book and cover design by Dawn Kresan. Typeset in Adobe Garamond Pro
and Edwardian Script, and printed offset on Rolland Natural at Coach
House Printing in Ontario, Canada. Edited by Aimée Parent Dunn.

Palimpsest Press would like to thank the Canada Council for the Arts, and
the Ontario Arts Council for their support of our publishing program. We
also acknowledge the assistance of the Government of Ontario through
the Ontario Book Publishing Tax Credit.

Library and Archives Canada Cataloguing in Publication

Lemay, Shawna, 1966–, author
    Rumi and the red handbag / Shawna Lemay.

ISBN 978-1-926794-26-6 (PBK.)

    I. TITLE.

PS8573.E5358R86 2015   C813'.54   C2015-901807-2

"I too am: is."

—Clarice Lispector, *A Breath of Life*

"Even mountains hang on strings. The 'isness' of things is miraculous: that there is something rather than nothing."

—John O'Donohue

I.s.

At sixteen, I tenderly resolved on my pseudonym. Shaya Neige. I knew I needed one if I were ever to write anything. Much later I discovered that this name, the last of the hundreds of possible autographs beginning with the sound of a hush, I would, with utmost seriousness, gently and savagely write in a notebook, was very close to the name Chaya, the name given to the author I most revere, Clarice Lispector, when she was born. A name she kept until she moved to Brazil.

There is a thing I do with names. I look for the secret in them. And maybe that is why I took the job at *Theodora's Fine Consignment Clothing* in the basement of the fusty brick building. I wanted to approach someone named Theodora, though it turned out there was no such person. I still like to think of her though and imagine her walking down the crumbling brick stairs, holding the surprisingly elaborate wrought iron railing. Gliding into the store with a Danish pastry in her hand or a vintage birdcage held high. But no. When I first walked into the store that winter day with my résumé, merely toying with the idea of working there, I met a young woman behind the counter. I was compelled to ask her name as I could see she was daydreaming, breathing the shallow mist of daydreams deeply into her small lungs. Lungs that, when she was younger, her doctor had x-rayed. She remembered him tapping, pointing at her illuminated lungs, saying—these are very undersized, undeveloped, strange.

Maybe for a short time I even thought of her as Theodora, but she was Ingrid-Simone Stephens. Never, I learned, just Ingrid, or just Simone, but Ingrid-Simone. I don't know whether she made up her own name or it was given, but she wrote her initials thus—I.s.

I will tell you straight away, you should know that I refuse to tell her story if the ending is sad. Like Macabea, there but for the grace of God go I, run over by a yellow Mercedes. Speaking of yellow, did I mention that Ingrid-Simone Stephens wore a bright yellow daisy in her hair the day I met her? The temperature was thirty degrees below, at least, and she had had a flower in her hair. The memory of a fresh flower in a young woman's hair at the beginning of an early winter has made me resolve that, in contrast to what I wrote before, this story will verge toward honesty.

I would get to know her slowly. Writing this, I will slowly get to know her. I reserve the right to tell myself this; I reserve the right to tamper with my fragile and trembling remembrances, with my often illegible notes. After I was hired, we were mostly left alone. We were alone, the two of us, that entire expansive winter, with its record cold spells and abundant snow. The owner of the store, whose name was actually Florine, received the consignments, the second-hand gowns and cocktail dresses, the blouses and scarves, the shoes and purses, in the rear of the building. She steamed the dresses and put them on a rack, pushing them, rolling free and headlong, out onto the floor. I looked after the dresses and most of the other clothes. Ingrid-Simone took hold of the accessories.

One day I came in just a couple of hours late due to a doctor's appointment. The clothes, which had previously been arranged by size, had all been moved and were now arranged by colour. I was stunned. The store was transformed. What had been a dingy mass of mournful discards was a singing glorious array. I laughed out loud when I walked into the store, stomping the snow from my salt-stained boots, my eyes wide. I twirled around arms out, quite incredulous, gaping at the lime greens, the reds, the oranges, and all the shades of blue. It felt tropical. Ingrid-Simone watched from the front desk, smiling. And she said, —you know I did that just to make you happy.

How did she know I was unhappy?

She was maybe twenty years old when we worked together at Theodora's and I felt for a while that I had joined her quest merely by watching from the sidelines. To hear her plan and dream, you see, helped to pass the long days. She was driven to take a journey and desperately wanted to visit the Museum of Bags and Purses in Amsterdam. Sometimes she seemed absurdly frantic when she talked about it.

—If I can't get there, I don't know what I'll do. Did you know that there's a handbag at the museum, covered entirely with peacock feathers? It's exquisite, I'm telling you, it's divine. If I could open that particular bag and breathe in its breath, that would be something. Rhapsody! I'm not saying they'd let me, but maybe I could have someone open it or tell me what was inside it when they brought it to the museum. They probably catalogue such things. Wouldn't you catalogue such things if you worked at the Museum of Bags and Purses? I'm sure there are lists and lists of things that came out of the museum's handbags. Maybe they leave some things in? Just for the sake of authenticity. Or to keep people wondering. Worn down lipsticks, their colourful peaks and valleys, the nerves and desires and bold confidence of the women who applied them. Humbug candies, maybe there are one or two of those in the black leather one shaped like a huge ocean liner, the Normandie, it is.

Ingrid-Simone had rescued a chaotic jewel-toned sequined evening bag that had arrived in the store and used that to collect her mad money, as she called it. Her interest in handbags was contagious, grave and exuberant, but I eventually found that her true obsession was the soul. "What is the soul?" asks Rumi, the poet. "I cannot stop asking. If I could taste one sip of an answer, I could break out of this prison for drunks." She quoted this to me, I, who has no memory for quotations but loves poetry. I asked her for quotes when the store was empty and she would hop up on the high front counter in her short black skirt, sitting with her netted legs dangling, and recite.

—The Rumi, I would say, and she obliged.

It was odd. I was mesmerised by this young woman immediately, the soft careful way she talked, slow and deliberate but chocolaty, smoky, you know, like a deep red wine—plummy. I had dropped out of a doctoral program and had internalized my identity as a failed scholar quickly. This new identity did something to me, compressed my spine, and all of the fear I harboured did not turn into fearlessness but rather an agitated despair. I often felt lost and dizzy and numb and stupid all in a rush. I became suddenly interested in all the nuances of my own dreams rather than with anything I had ever read, I was liquid where before I had been solid. And here was this eloquent and passionate woman, largely unschooled, who perhaps had a better sense of how to seek and compile and delve than I ever had. For I feared improper tangents, going off rapt for long stretches in the wrong direction, wasting time. For Ingrid-Simone, the idea of hoarding thoughts, holding so many threads of ideas like cupped water as you knelt, knees grinding into finest gravel, thirsty by a mountain stream, did not terrify or oppress but instead exhilarated her.

I knew I would always be distant from her, but this distance was immediate and irrevocably intimate, filling me with the most intense apprehension for random instants. I was being born in her vibrant and remote presence, rising up awkwardly into the quiet swan of myself and no one saw it. This birthing was somnolent, unreachable, and yet profound and mysterious. I felt elegant, sublime. She had a nonchalant way of accepting, not just who I was, but also who I was becoming. I felt engulfed by a joyous inebriate inhalation. Did I imagine such things? Such feelings? I felt I had become part of a prayer, or a mantra, or a few bars of a Chopin prelude.

She was so young and so calm. Occasionally I thought I saw glimpses of myself in her, but I, I have always been nervous, skittish, timorous. I had been researching my dissertation all summer, that expansive, luscious, green summer before I came to Theodora's, the summer before I fled. Before I chickened out, as one colleague named this act of surrender. The topic, which I was yet refining, was the secrets of women writers, and by extension, the secrets of women characters in literature. I was trying to find the connections between the two. I had difficulty narrowing down which writers, but this paled compared to the problem of writing about secrets. Sometimes they were revealed, sometimes they were hinted at, but often it was just something I felt in my bones.

I was overwhelmed by how well women could conceal things, hide and cover tracks, by how very elusive they could be. There were the public secrets, the ones let out of birdcages painted white. And juicy ones too, that were used, maybe subconsciously, to hide other ineluctable secrets, smaller more precious and damning secrets.

I compiled lists of known secrets: Charlotte Brontë's unrequited love. The toothache she had had when she began writing Jane Eyre. The two diaries that Anais Nin kept: red for Henry Miller, green for her husband, Hugh. And I thought a lot about burned or destroyed letters and—their potential secrets—Jane Austen's letters burned selectively by her sister Cassandra, for example. Scholars surmise that the author of *Sense and Sensibility* had, at points, described an illness with a rather unbecoming precision.

I also compiled lists of possible secrets: Affairs. Unrequited love. Children given up for adoption. Hidden sexual orientation. Yearnings. Leanings. Lapses. Injuries inflicted. Unrealized dreams. Skeletons in the closet. I also thought about the changing nature of secrets. How our modern sensibilities cause us to react differently to secrets when found out. We are not so easily shocked by them now. But still, they are kept.

The idea of betraying these secrets once discovered, once intuited and scraped out of dark places, out of carefully hidden spots, contributed to my collapse, my flight.

I was dealing with the personal repercussions of having left the university, of the label 'ABD,' of feeling that I had betrayed an institution and my soul. My psychic discomposure was taking up residence in the pores of my skin. I was nakedly visible and yet felt dispirited, as though I were disappearing. And yet.

I considered going back, knowing that I couldn't. I considered carrying on writing about the secrets of women writers and literary characters from the 18th to 20th centuries through a framework of genetic criticism —the branch of criticism that looks at authorial intention via the DNA of a manuscript, its origins in scribbles, strikeouts, and marginalia, and the layers of the writing itself. I was interested in the genesis of the text, the soul of it, you could say. The rough draft, the handwritten text. The glimpses into a nascent state were thrilling to me. The study of genetic criticism, it has been said, is the study of writing in the process of being born. I was drawn to the scribble, those marks which indicate the pause of the pen or pencil. A thought, being formed, the hand poised above the page. Signs of the writer. At such moments, you feel more connected to the writer than you ordinarily would while reading their work. Scientific and at times merely descriptive on the surface, this type of scholarship had a magical force that drew me to it.

I considered writing this from outside the institution, outside the academy. I imagined myself just finding out the facts, making lists of the marks I found, notating them, and writing nothing. I wanted to know, really, if I was capable of keeping secrets. And I was worried I would find out too much or that there were, after all, no secrets of the sort that I posited. Or that perhaps all of my hunches and scant evidence was a sign of my own madness. So maybe, maybe, with all this roiling in my head, it was difficult for me to see that Ingrid-Simone herself was carrying a secret.

Who doesn't, of course, carry secrets, a pouch of butterfly wings, or paper burned in a fire, the dark flesh rising up from a bonfire in the middle of summer. Some you forget are secrets, having no one to reveal them to anyway. Like how I first met Florine, the owner of this second-hand emporium full of battered cocktail dresses, hawked plumes, outgrown gowns, everything verging on très unfashionable. Had she remembered and kept this secret to herself too, or had she not recognized me?

I used to take extremely long, solitary walks. I walked out to meet my loneliness, to take care of it, to speak with it rhythmically and gently, as one would rock a baby. I would strike out from the university that fall, when I had begun to contemplate bolting from those halls. Once, I found myself at the edge of the city, by a highway and a narrow stretch of farmland. There were huge rounds of hay, freshly baled. The scent from them was heaven. Yes, I was that sentimental, I imagined heaven had a corner that smelled just like fresh mown hay and I stood with my back to one for quite a while, drinking bottled water from the pouch I had slung over my shoulder, just breathing in the clover and timothy. When I looked up, for I must have closed my eyes or been so deep within my reveries, I didn't see the bicycle until it was nearly upon me. Nor was I completely visible to the cyclist. A woman was pedalling in a standing position on the dirt trail, wobbling on the strict unevenness. A faint cloud of dust arose. She was wearing a lumberjack shirt and a white scarf on her head. She seemed to have arrived from another time and place, the 1950s maybe, near a small town. Even the bicycle was from some other era, having no gears, no fancy gadgets. Maybe there was a silver bell. The bicycle was blue with a white flourish for the chain guard. I think she wouldn't have stopped but my presence against the hay bale surprised her and set her off balance.

And though she was surprised, she said, I'm sure she said, —Hello, my name is Maureen. How pleasant it is today, and added, unhurriedly, softly, as though she were speaking to a child clasping a bouquet of daisies, —I love riding in this field, sometimes I'll see deer and coyotes.

—Do you live near here? I asked her.

She floated her hand vaguely and said, —Not really. Then we went our own ways, me following her for a bit, watching her struggle, wobble, and pedal on the dusty trail before taking the exit that led into the suburbs, back to the busy road with the convenience store, where I would buy a solemnly cold bottle of cream soda, something I hadn't had since I was a child.

I thought of it as the Cream Soda Day. And I often found myself wondering about Maureen, who she was, where she had come from and how she seemed so much at home in that field, in herself. I kept thinking about the softness of her eyes, the checked flannel shirt, the way she seemed to welcome me into the field. I remember the puff of dust that followed her when she departed. Staring at the dust, watching it settle, long after she had disappeared. I remember thinking she rode the bicycle as though she were wearing glass slippers; the glass, I imagined, was millefiori.

When I arrived for my interview months later at Theodora's, I recognized her, shocked, but I said nothing because she said nothing. What could one say? I thought, dust settling, I thought, cream soda. I was yet breathing the reluctant and relieved escape of dust and old paper of the beloved library I had given up. Had I given it up, walked away? Was the library still breathing me? I felt as though I had been on a respirator and the library had been my source of air, that my obscure and delicious research supplied my blood with necessary oxygen. I adored these puppy breaths I could not comprehend, was not asked to comprehend. I had not factored in this loss, this bereavement, into the possible effects of my escape.

&

Even at the beginning, Ingrid-Simone told me of her discoveries, breathily surreptitious, waiting for the store to be empty, for the racks to stop their swaying, or for a woman heaped up with garments to try on, some of which were guaranteed to be ill-fitting, and which would occupy a decent amount of time. Ingrid-Simone always tossed in some matching shoes and draped cheap necklaces and bangles over the heavy curtain, winking at me over her shoulder. She would then withdraw a small notebook, no larger than a pat of butter, from her cleavage. She had a strange talent for writing elegantly in an incredibly tiny but perfectly legible hand. This was not a feat as far as she was concerned and she never allowed me to make anything of it at all.

"The word 'soul' is an immortal word," says Gaston Bachelard. "In certain poems it cannot be effaced, for it is a word born of our breath."

—Is not that amazing? The word 'soul' I've always felt is exactly like breath. You don't say it like a breath but you feel it as one. You think it as breath. The word soul in your head is a breath. Does that make sense?

—Yes, I found myself saying to her, —yes. And I thought: how does she know Bachelard? I had barely heard of Bachelard. How did she know to hold the word soul in her mouth, in her head, so?

☙

Ingrid-Simone was responsible for the accessories that came into the store. Piles of shoes that needed scuffed bottoms washed or faux jewels that needed polishing. She also undertook a task I could not, not having the stomach for the grit and residue of others, of going through the boxes of purses that Florine would, sighing and shaking her head, dump unceremoniously on the counter behind the front desk. She cleaned the exterior first, saving the interior for last. Savouring, she said, the moment when she opened the purse. It was a torture she allowed herself, a sigh's benediction.

—Every purse has its own, you know. Each one opens with a particular, though somehow familiar, exhalation. A puff, a grand dilapidated and sometimes obscure sigh. The scent of eucalyptus lozenges, or peppermint, or a powdery perfume. Sometimes there is a fragrant mossy scent. Foresty.

Sometimes, pure sour cough. And here she said the word cough with just the hint of a cough.

Quickly I became fond of her without meaning to, though I constantly encouraged myself to stay detached from everyone and everything in this store full of castoffs and whatsoever is fleeting. I would not let her meet with any yellow Mercedes. It occurred to me early on that she was trying to tell me as much as possible. She was spilling things out, unexpected things, as though just realizing how stuffed full she was and how no one would be saving what she held dear, what could be held dear. I put my hands out. I laced my fingers tightly together so the offerings would not slip through.

She talked in a way that dying mothers, dying young, talk to their children. I had seen videos mothers with terminal cancer make for their small children, on talk shows, and had had my heart broken at three in the afternoon. How intently I listened to Ingrid-Simone, not least because I felt that this act—listening, listening itself—could prevent any possible collisions. I could fend off cars, if need be, herds of them.

Was it dictation? A dictation of the soul? She was handing herself to me, the way you hand someone a tissue out of your purse, digging down, grasping the package in your hand, and drawing out triumphantly the cloudy tissue, waving it a second, airing it out.

I returned home at the end of the day and tried to capture this—her sweetness, for that is what came through. Everything I could remember, I wrote down. I became more adept, more fluent, an unsanctioned amanuensis. Did I ask permission to do such things? I was only doing this to sort things out in my head, I told myself. And then the more I wrote down *her*, the more I remembered myself at that age. I got carried away and wrote down things I might have been thinking at her age, fifteen years ago. How could I not remember what I was thinking fifteen years ago? Why had I not recorded them then? Would she remember herself at this age? And failing to remember, perhaps I could at some future point bestow upon her my recordings with their increasingly ample liberties edited out.

I talked myself into believing that I wasn't stealing but preserving. I imagined the nice paper on which I would type up and print off the notes I took, the Japanese paper I would use for the cover, the ribbon I would use to bind it all. Yes, I infringed, embellished, but if I couldn't quite remember myself at twenty, would she? I would hand it over in a handmade box and talk of rough sketches, smudges and debris, and the conjunction of artist and thief.

I was fifteen years older than Ingrid-Simone and yet I thought of her as a daughter, though we as easily could have been sisters. Yes, she was a daughter. The love I felt was daughter-love, rather than sister-love. I knew this though I had had neither sister nor daughter. For her to have been my daughter, my real daughter, I would have been seventeen years old when she arrived on this earth with its blue sky and swirling clouds, the skies of so many different colours. I wondered what the sky was like when she was born. What the scene was she saw through the window when her mother first showed her the great outdoors- I imagined people did such things. Showed their newborns how glorious things are, despite how narrow and confined and limited our view happens to be. That nevertheless there is a chance, a window, and sometimes a bird will fly by, maybe the miracle of a hummingbird or a bumblebee or a dragonfly or a leaf. So there are surprises just like that, too.

⁊

I often walked in the door of my apartment and, without taking off my shoes or my snow-damp winter coat, sat in the nubby turquoise armchair with dulled silver legs and took out the pad of large sticky notes from my bag and began writing. On a cerulean-blue sticky note, I wrote: she remembers names with blistering accuracy, names of ordinary people. People that appear in news stories, good Samaritans, the victim of a break and enter, an elderly woman who fell on the ice, a child who raises money for Tsunami relief. Martin Colrain. Martha O'Hara. Fabiana Levesque. All these she'll remember. And even the customers in the store. She would read their names from a credit card and hand it back, thanking them by name, sincerely. Looking in their eyes. And a week later she would say, —remember Sandra Edmondson, who bought the lilac organza floor-length a couple of weeks ago? This evening bag would go perfectly. And she would dreamily outline the embroidery, lazily opening and closing the clasp, twisting and untwisting the round metal pieces in her fingers, rubbing them as though they were a crystal ball.

❧

Ingrid-Simone had the habit of softly beginning —hmmmmm. Hmm, she would say, and pause. As if pondering, or saying a mantra, somewhere between the two.

❧

Once, I came upon her at lunch. That is, I went looking for her, ran out with bare arms, leaving the store empty, taking the stairs in twos, and found her in the nearby coffee shop where she was sitting in the window, reading. She had forgotten to return to the store that unseasonably warm winter day, absorbed in what she called a vintage Harlequin romance. She had bought a huge armful of them at Value Village. I would have been embarrassed. Too embarrassed to read a romance in public, the reflection of the cover overlapping, doubling, wobbling, face onto face, décolletage concealing décolletage, the title repeating itself one line down in bright yellow in the frosted, dripping, sunny window for all to see as they walked by. I would have been embarrassed that I had fallen into the well of such a book and forgotten where I was supposed to be. Had I mentioned this,

Ingrid-Simone might have said something like, —well, however are we to know precisely at any one moment in time what that means, *where you're supposed to be*. Certainly she did not appear discomfited when I came to retrieve her, pulling her reluctantly from the story. I could see it was an effort for her to stop reading.

—Oh, I know they're stupid. But they're so, hmm, impossible, you know? That it's possible to believe, and also... Hmm. They set up an ache that is warm and perversely fulfilling. To know it's impossible, anything that perfect, so well orchestrated, so full of coincidences. Silly. Whoever wrote the book must understand, at least, that however simple we are, this need to feel loved, we're not alone in that. It's a way to manage heartache too I think. You can let it out in dribbles and rein it back in just as the heroes have to rein in their passions at some point in the narrative. Captivating really, the collective energy that must be created, all these women sitting in their rooms writing these, for years and years, for decades, producing romances, so many of them. And then, all the women in turn reading them, just devouring them. Focusing on this one type of plot. Which so often seems to involve a Jane Eyre character and a male love interest slowly coming to recognize who the protagonist really is, when even she doesn't quite know it herself. I suppose that is what overwhelms me. The sheer quantity of silence surrounding this moment, of identifying with this character who feels she will never be understood, knows it so thoroughly. Never be recognized. But then, but then, she is. She is. And besides, I want to know what they're all going through. All these millions of women who read these things. What are they going through that they read these like candy?

—Hmm. And all those people who automatically disparage romances, I don't trust them, you know? What are they afraid of? The small fantasies of millions of women? I wonder.

—I admit that what I really like about them is that they stop, they end, right at the moment before all the real things in life happen. I'm free to imagine blissful lives for them, even if sometimes I can't. I appreciate the ones that have epilogues. What a lovely idea. Those are the romance authors I admire—they don't leave things to chance. I once read a romance that had the most detailed epilogue. There was every certainty that those characters were going to be happy for generations. Generations! How sublime. How comforting!

Then she stood and wrapped herself slowly in her tweedy brown floor-length winter coat. She stood and I waited. Then we ran back to the store in the cold because I was wearing a dress, my plain grey dress that day, with lime green tights, and I hadn't taken the time to drag out my coat to come find Ingrid-Simone, languishing with her crumbling book. The pages were even disintegrating as she read, falling out, the glue holding the book together eroding. When we got back to the store she got out a large elastic band and wrapped it around the book, which hid the noses of hero and heroine. I noticed the illustration of the woman; this must have been a cover from the 1970s. She had a crown of wild yellow daisies woven into her hair, which was loose and tumbling and waving, as all hair does for such women. This reminded me of Ingrid-Simone, though she didn't at all look like this.

—Just imagine, that we are so often standing beside someone, hmm, say, in the grocery store or at the bus stop, and they are, well, full, so full, just brimming with small fantasies and dreams. Isn't that interesting?

I thought I should point out the work being done by academics on the romance novel, their studies of gender inequities, empowerment, narrative re-inscriptions, societal codes, and patriarchal discourse. We could have talked about the ways in which women portrayed other women or the history of the romance novel. But it was as though she were under a spell cast by her escape into this decrepit novel, into thoughts of imminent rescue, of being known and understood and cherished, and I was drawn into that spell somehow as well. Or I was reluctant to break hers.

Back at the store, Ingrid-Simone polished an entire box of tangled vintage necklaces we had received that morning. Costume jewellery, it was once called. She told me she liked to take the bus to the University after work some days. To the Humanities library. Usually, she took the elevator right up to the fifth floor where all the books of literature and criticism are shelved. Other days she sought out the art books, or philosophy books.

—It's so interesting, everyone knows I'm not a student, I can tell. They look at me so oddly. Maybe it's because I'm glowing. I feel like I'm emanating, oh, I don't know what. But there are colours swirling all around me, because I know I'm about to find something. Saffron and turquoise, honestly, and then sometimes a sort of Venetian pink. It's very beautiful. The library brings that out in me.

—Anyway. What I do is I find a carrel that has a stack of books left in it. I never use the computer to find books. Sometimes I go to the shelves and wander through and see if any books fall out as I walk by. This really happens, honestly. Once a book fell right into my arms and I cradled it all the way to my carrel, nervously, worried that it might disappear.

—Last night though, I read the most interesting book. I can't remember the author's name. Which is a pity, because I would like to look at this book again someday. I'm sure it will find me. Here is the thing she said that I keep repeating in my head: that she must write "as beautifully as love." It made me wish I could write, you know? If I could write, oh, as beautifully as love. Of course, then I was thinking that maybe this thought was not entirely incompatible with what occurs in my crumbling pulp romances, my cotton-candy books. Of course, it's not entirely compatible either, the writing is so syrupy and silly. But the intention, the intention. Is it possible, do you think, to live as beautifully as love?

She said all this, drawing out the syllables as Audrey Hepburn might have, here and there, as she polished and untangled, her head at an angle.

If Vermeer had painted her at this moment, he would have captured the face of a young woman, both wounded and serene. He would have painted the mound of glitz, the rhinestones and the gold and silver chains, and with just a few flicks of the brush, cobalt, ruby, indigo, emerald, he would have indicated the entanglement, the slender fingers imprisoned, so gently, softly. Maybe there would have been the slightest indication of those colours she feels swirling around her. Saffron, Venetian Pink, turquoise.

&

I was never able to wear second-hand clothes, truth be told. There, I said it. I suppose that sounds strange. But I found they held too much of the person who wore them previously. I felt that the moment I tried a sweater on in the store, no matter how lovely it was, no matter how pristine, I felt various things—sometimes unhappiness, at other times smugness, self-righteousness. I didn't want any of it on me, the film of these grimy states of being. The terrible sadnesses, the mistakes, the abandonments. Sometimes I felt illness, or death, or despair. I suppose there was also happiness, joy, but that was more difficult to sense, I don't know why. There was a residue of the places the previous owner had travelled, a smudge of the struggles they had had, of people they had embraced, a scent of the rooms they had lived in, however softly, however fearfully or belligerently or even kindly. The complications, the attachments, overwhelmed me. Intolerable. I could not drape myself in them.

Once, I broke this rule and bought a heavily beaded scarf unlike anything I had ever seen. The fabric was tangerine on one side and the beads were fuchsia and buttercup and seashell pink. Flowers and little birds and stars. I wore it out to a restaurant one evening. I met a friend from the English department, the one person who didn't think I was making a dreadful mistake by quitting or try to talk me into going back and completing my degree, and who didn't mind being in the company of one who was so unfinished. We sipped some sparkling wine and were about to make a toast to the unfinished, to the abandoned, to the deliriously courageous, a toast to following your bliss, a line from Joseph Campbell that has made it onto fridge magnets and t-shirts and decorative pillows. A line we subsequently laughed about, since working in a second-hand clothing store was not exactly what I would call following my bliss and had more to do with paying the rent.

Nevertheless, I was enjoying the bubbles, when a woman walked up behind me and laid her hand at first lightly on the back of my neck, on the scarf, then tightened like a bird claw, and said, —this, as she picked up an end and let it trail through the fingers of her other hand, —belonged to my mother, may she rest in peace. She came around, then, and I saw her, her skin pulled tight, obscenely tanned in winter, with a vulgarity about the way she was dressed.

—You bought it at Theodora's, she said.

—Yes, I replied.

—Good! She uttered with gusto and walked away in a slow motion swirl. Was it good? I never wore it again without feeling her strong, old hand on my neck. My overactive imagination conjured up thoughts of the woman having killed her mother, tightening the scarf around her mother's neck with those taloned hands of hers.

The city was not so large; I could see this sort of thing happening all the time. These encounters. Oh, maybe the previous owner wouldn't always say something but there would be looks. The feelings I had wouldn't go away, not even after several washings, so I gave up on buying sweaters and certainly scarves.

Ingrid-Simone didn't share my squeamishness. She had a knack for putting brilliant outfits together. For dressing entirely in second-hand clothes and somehow making them all seem new and vivid as though she had stepped off a London runway.

—Where did you get that dress? I asked her. She was wearing a lilac cotton and lace dress over seemingly expensive tattered jeans with high heels and a long, thin scarf patterned with a field of spring flowers around her swan-like neck.

—Oh, very funny, she said. When she realized I was serious, she said, —from here silly, from here, of course. It came in last week in the same batch as all the lilac clothes. Remember the woman who was divesting of her lilac, smoke-infested wardrobe? Yes, I did. We had called it the 'lilac smoke collection.' No amount of steaming and freshening could expunge the scent, deeply held in the garments, but somehow Ingrid-Simone had purged the odour from her dress. On Ingrid-Simone, the colour deepened, had a smokier hue, more mysterious than when all the lilacs had hung on the rack together.

In this way, she was someone new each day. One day she wore a grunge inspired, bohemian outfit; the next, her outfit was inspired by the 1950s with a pencil skirt, fitted jacket, pillbox hat, gloves. And yet another, she arrived wearing a black shirt, skinny black pants and black pointy flats with white socks, exactly like Audrey Hepburn in the movie *Funny Face*, where she had danced in a jazz club in Paris. To know Ingrid-Simone was to surrender to her many possibilities. I often thought a picture ought to be taken every morning of the way she dressed and how she breezed in through the door, or entered slowly, cat-like, or briskly, or swishily, or as though afraid someone was following her. Capturing each outfit combined with the way she entered the store, that would be a work of art of some importance.

❧

—Exactly why did you leave the university? Ingrid-Simone asked the next day. As I tried to explain, my reasons became all tied up in knots, though at the same time they began to clarify a little for me. There's hardly ever just one reason for doing something that is both so small in the grand scheme, but monumental, in the life of one person. Maybe at the core, I felt fraudulent, or perhaps the academic process seemed fraudulent. The idea, perhaps, that one person can teach another person how to live, how to read this life of ours, even if through novels and poems, seemed illogical or misleading. In the end, after obtaining my degree, I would have had to sell myself as a teacher, more than as a scholar or researcher, which is how I saw myself. Teaching would include revealing those literary secrets I didn't feel privy to, or secrets which were not my own to tell. Teaching included putting novels on the stand and questioning them until the truth was wrung from them. Until a confession was extracted.

The same day she asked, though her question was more of a soft accusation, —you must have a secret? Playful, she was never impolite and would never directly ask a question so personal. In that second, I understood that if she had asked me point blank, —What secret do you keep? I, like any good secret keeper, would lie.

Secrets, anyway, are usually incidental. How you keep one is important, how you choose to live with it, let it alter you, matters. Perhaps it makes you a kinder person, someone more willing to forgive and understand. Secrets have that potential.

෨

Neither of us had been working at the store all that long the morning we came in, both of us walking up the street from opposite directions at exactly the same time, to find Florine wasn't there. I vividly recall Ingrid-Simone jiggling her key in the front door lock. We were cold and the door had a layer of frost on it, as did the round metal lock. Ingrid-Simone took the key out and breathed on it, huffing, trying to warm it. There was an ice fog in the air, an unusual dampness.

—Maybe we should go round the back and ask Florine to let us in, I said. But Ingrid-Simone gave me a look that said, patience my love, and repeated the procedure a few more times. I humoured her, remaining silent, not believing this could work.

But it did work and we were in, suddenly warm and not a bit giddy, me congratulating her on the use of her superpower, the ability to thaw ancient lock mechanisms with her warm breath, and she laughed, sparkling, and said how full of hot air she was, proven once and for all. And we both admired the frost that had attached itself to the hair around our faces once we took our woolly hats off.

—We're angels, she said, —beautiful snow fairies, look at us! And we flipped our tresses about while the frost disappeared, and our hair was damp and rather limp.

—Let's hope we don't have any ex-boyfriends come into the store today, I said, and she looked at me, actually shocked, and walked away. I meant to tease her about boyfriends later to see what her reaction meant but had no chance and the thought slipped away.

The closet in the back room where we hung our things was dark. Usually Florine turned the lights on for us when she arrived. No Florine? We looked at each other. First thing in the morning, she was always there, in silence, sorting clothes or sometimes doing paperwork, organizing the consignment invoices, paying bills, writing numbers down in a ledger since she refused to use the computer. More often, she was hanging out the back door at the bottom of the narrow stairwell, one foot in, having a cigarette. When she saw we had arrived, she would bend down and put the cigarette out in an old black saucer of an ashtray, usually quite full, that she left sitting outside the back door.

Later in the day she would often disappear, quite randomly. Maybe she went for long walks, or long lunches with unknown ladies, we never knew and she certainly never said. Sometimes she came back looking as though she had engaged in strenuous exercise, all flushed and mussed and damp. Exhausted looking. At other times she would have leaves in her hair, snow clinging to her boots and the back of her down coat, and we surmised quietly that she had walked into the ravine, laid down, and made snow angels. Or was having a clandestine affair. We would ask her, —did you have a nice lunch out? And she would sputter —oh, lunch, nononono. I brought a sandwich. Going to eat it now. The sun is bright today. Then she would walk away from us, go to the back room and hang out the cold back door with her cigarettes.

But that morning, she wasn't there, and we thought maybe her key hadn't worked very well either. So we swung open the back door and Ingrid-Simone got her key out to see if it would work and it did. There was a skiff of snow and no footprints. We closed the door.

—She's probably just late. I hope nothing happened. One of us said these things and then we shrugged and went on with the opening duties of vacuuming the rug, setting up the cash register, unlocking the front door, and turning the open sign over. We expected a slow day thanks to the weather. Ingrid-Simone sat on the front counter, as no one was in the store, and took out her miniature notebook filled with her miniature writing. She flipped a few pages until she found what she wanted.

She read, —"Run your fingers through my soul. For once, just once, feel exactly what I feel, believe what I believe, perceive as I perceive, look, experience, examine, and for once, just once, understand." This is by Anonymous. How lovely, lovely! Don't you think? Run your fingers through my soul! Okay, it's a bit corny too, I admit. Do you believe in the soul? Last night I Googled the word, 'soul,' and I suppose it's no surprise but there are millions of results, utterly millions!

There was a rack of clothes needing to be put away from the day before. I took one or two pieces off the rack and held them up to me and danced around while Ingrid-Simone chattered away from her perch, scrunching her face or laughing occasionally at my clumsy, faux-elegant dance. Once in a while she stopped and said, —oh, yes, now that one, that's really you, darling. Usually these were the supremely ridiculous dresses, worth a fortune but gaudy as hell. We talked about pitying the person who bought a particular garment, and took to saying, —O, I pity that one, which was later just shortened to, —Pity!

—Pity! She called out, as I twirled around the store, and then she asked, —do you believe the soul is composed of parts? How many do you reckon?

I replied, quite cavalierly, —run your fingers through my soul and find out…

—No, no, I mean, look, look. The Stoics, whoever they were, thought the soul had eight distinct parts. Eight! They thought the soul was like a breath, too. Others describe it as a flame. Heraclitus. Her-a-cli-tus. He thought it was a flame. A nourishing flame. I've written this down, nourishing flame, breath. The soul moves with an exquisite fluency, I've copied that as well. I don't know what any of it means, I realize that. But do you believe there is life after death? Do you believe a soul could follow another soul, haunt one? Or accompany one? With an exquisite fluency?

I realized she was serious, her voice becoming suddenly sombre, downcast and low.

The telephone rang, disturbing the moment. Funny, I suppose, how things unfold. But that day, at least, unwound around the moment of the phone, the ringing, its sharp interruption and the news it brought. Even if that is true, the importance of such ringings, I worry that I have not yet explained fully enough the strangeness and naivety of Ingrid-Simone, her freshness. She was like someone from a Woody Allen movie but that does not do her justice, for she was real, utterly and poignantly and delightfully real. I want to compare her to wildflowers but that's too easy.

What shaped a person like Ingrid-Simone? Though maybe what I mean to ask is, what shaped a poem like Ingrid-Simone? Until the day of the ringing, I didn't ask myself this question. I only wanted to watch, as one might watch a movie, to see what would happen next, to understand what each of her gestures meant as an insight into her largely unknowable character.

I can still conjure that particular ring in my head, I swear. Ingrid-Simone picked up the receiver and held it at an angle from her ear so I could also hear. The voice from the dead, saying, —I will not be there. I will not... be... there. And the sound of the hanging up, the loud tone on the line gone dead.

We had suspected as much. Florine would not come into the store that day. But we were also reminded that there were many things we didn't know about Florine. Did we know anything? We pooled our scant knowledge of her. We started by wondering if she were ill. Or if she was hungover. This seemed too scandalous; we laughed and put our hands over our open mouths. It seemed impossible. Then Ingrid-Simone suggested in a more subdued tone that Florine sounded as though she were drugged. Sleeping pills, we speculated. Or too much Nyquil. Yes, that was it, she had a cold and took Nyquil and felt groggy, like death warmed over. That sounded right.

Should we take her anything? Was there anyone to look after her? We didn't know her phone number, let alone where she lived. She never spoke of a partner, or husband, or even of a very good friend. We were awful! Instantly filled with guilt. Embarrassed. We rummaged in the front desk for something that might have her telephone number on it, a contact list. Her last name, what was her last name? Surely we knew that.

I told Ingrid-Simone the story of how I was sure I had seen Florine in the field at the edge of the city riding a bike, an antique Schwinn. How I imagined stories about her. How neither of us mentioned having met before when I came to the store for the interview. How I might have even come up with strange theories about twins or doppelgangers, except that once I heard her talking in a low tone to a woman who came in holding a bicycle helmet under her arm. I heard the odd phrase, a few words here and there. Florine had said, —my Schwinn, more than once.

We became quite serious for the rest of the day, quiet. We dropped all of the "run your fingers through my soul" business. There were very few customers so we had long expanses of silence, which was unusual for us. Florine didn't come in the next day either or the following one.

Late in the afternoon on the third day of Florine's absence, Ingrid-Simone was tidying the handbags when she heard a rattle. She opened a worn and black handbag, very much like a doctor's bag, and retrieved a smooth stone, shaped like a heart.

—So odd! How could I have missed this? I couldn't have missed it, I'm very thorough, I know I am. Someone must have come into the store and placed it inside. But that's absurd. What sort of person would do such a weird thing? I mean, it seems like something I might do, but who else would? It seems like a message.

When Ingrid-Simone said the word 'weird', it was as though she were handing out the highest of compliments, she said it with such awe, with so much air before the w. I had never heard anyone say the word the way she said it. It didn't sound the way people said it in the 1970s —she said it in an utterly modern way. Full of her breath, beginning with a whoosh, full of wonder and encompassing the esteem that she felt for anyone who was weird.

As we locked up that night, we decided to call the police the next day if Florine didn't call or appear. Though what we would tell them, we were unsure. We didn't know her last name or anything really. We would look ridiculous, daft.

But she did come in. The light was on in the dim back room when we arrived. The faint smell of cigarette smoke drifted to the front of the store, and there was Florine, hovering by the back door attempting to blow her smoke outside into the frigid air and watching it be repelled by the wall of cold, easing itself back inside. The first thing she did was wave us away. We left her. Went on with our opening duties. Opened the door. There was no one waiting to get in, as there were so many days. I volunteered to go to the back and talk to Florine. All I could get out of her that day was that she had not been ill. —No, nothing terminal, she joked. How exhausted she looked and her skin seemed grey. I thought she moved like a skeleton, as if she were part bird. I noticed that her hair was becoming increasingly grey. Had it been that streaked through before?

The rest of the winter, we attempted to learn more about her but after this day, she became more elusive. She would often be late. She disappeared during the day for long periods without telling us that she was leaving or when she arrived back. When Ingrid-Simone once boldly asked her to let us know when she was coming or going, so that if someone phoned for her we could tell them the appropriate thing, she just said, —message, take a message. And kept muttering, —yes, take a message. If someone calls asking, oh never mind, a message.

I returned to Ingrid-Simone, then, content that Florine was not in any immediate harm. And we hid between racks of clothes and talked and wondered. And made it a goal to find out as soon as we could, at least, what her name was, where she lived, and what her telephone number might be.

—I feel like a private investigator, or a snoop, or a peeping Tom. Maybe we'll have to follow her home. Have a stakeout! It would be for her own good, of course.

We planned a surveillance of Florine, which we never imagined enacting.

The day that Florine returned, I remember she rolled out a rack of freshly steamed clothes with a rather pointed look at the two of us that said: what am I paying you for, to hang out whispering amid the cocktail dresses? With her arms like skeleton wings unfurling rather magnificently, sublimely decrepit, she heaved a huge box of purses and shoes onto the counter behind the front desk for Ingrid-Simone and headed for the back room, arms flapping, stretching out I suppose, limbering up. We buried our heads immediately, exchanging a couple of looks, raised eyebrows and the like, for the next while. But eventually we ended up distracted, looking after one customer then another until we wound up whispering amid the lime green shawls and orange t-shirt dresses. We started talking again about finding out her name, her full name. Florine was not a popular name of late, maybe there was a way to search first names in a particular city, I wondered aloud. And then I said, —the only other person I've heard of with that name was a New York artist named Florine Stettheimer who painted interiors of parties and people and flowers all in an eccentric, modern, fantastic mode. Her palette was somewhat pastel and stomach churning, yet beautifully artificial, eclectic, and full of the drollness of a secluded socialite life. Her sister Carrie made a dollhouse that's in the New York City Museum. I saw it once, behind Plexiglas. Strange.

Ingrid-Simone wanted to know more about the dollhouse. The miniature paintings in it, originals done by artists like Marcel Duchamp. A miniature *Nude Descending a Staircase.* All the tiny period furniture. Sculptures even.

—Fascinating! I'm going to go to the library tonight and look up pictures.

A week after we talked about miniatures I received the first purse. I was wearing an orange dress.

༼

I, who in my whole life had never even dreamed of wearing an orange dress, wore the dream of an orange dress to work. An orange, beautifully cut, wrap-around dress swinging just below my knees. As an academic, even the pretend one I was, I could never have worn such a garment to the university. Not that anyone would have blinked. What you wore was not a factor, and so usually, students and professors on campus usually dressed in an understated mode. Not that there wasn't a certain amount of stylishness but it was a stylishness of a different sort altogether. You simply didn't wear attention-grabbing orange dresses when you wished to be unobserved. And all I had wanted to do was blend in and listen. I had wanted to listen. That calling, amid the others.

Maybe the combination of finding the heart-shaped stone in the handbag and the discussion of miniatures, or maybe Ingrid-Simone thinking in a way that was miniature, like her writing, led her to create the first tiny purse. Which is not to say that she thought small but that her thoughts were condensed, they required a certain amount of squinting, they brought attention to things that could just barely be seen. They examined what others might pass by or dismiss as inconsequential, a smudge, a blur, a randomness. Once she told me she was interested in graffiti, miniature graffiti. She found surfaces on which she could write quotations with her superfine markers. And she signed her graffiti—I.s.

—There's something I want to give you. Hmm. I want you to have it because of everything you give me, everything you teach me. Just being with you I feel like I'm growing, you know? I want you to have it. What it is, is, well, it's a purse sculpture I guess you could call it.

She held a small box on the palm of her hand, outstretched. I protested. —Honestly, honestly, what ever do I give you? Oh you're lovely, but no, I'm nothing.

—No, no, Shaya, I want you to have it, I made it for you.

And she smiled her really beautiful, soft, bemused smile that transformed her face into music; it was as though you could hear the string section come in. An opening up. A smile you could walk into as you would into a clearing in the forest. The light coming into the mossy space through the green leaves, golden and twinkling and pretty dappled.

She slid the box from the palm of her hand into the palm of mine, as though we were transferring a handful of pearls or a kitten. Yes, more like a kitten, calico because I like the sound of that word. The box was purring. I thought it must contain a breathing, purring, content life.

It was difficult to open. I was swallowed perfectly by that moment. Hypnotized by every particle of the purring gift. By the transfer, by her slightly chipped candy-apple red nail polish, the smudged and faded ink remnants of a reminder to herself on her wrist, by the shape of her hand as it was cupped, by the giving, by the shyness and boldness and girlish procedure. It seemed a magic trick—voila! presto! Suddenly the box lay in my hands, also cupped. So few are the times in my life when I can say I was thrilled by such an inner shiver of delight, I mean truly thrilled. How often we just throw such words about to cover up disappointments, things not coming up to expectations, but here I was intently and thoroughly thrilled. This was an unnatural state for me, so often inhibited and silent.

The lid removed, I couldn't see what was inside. I had a moment of blindness. So emotional and with no idea what I'd see, I briefly, for an instant, saw nothing. A darkness, which was just a film of water covering my eyes. I had to blink and blink and squint to behold.

I beheld. A miniature buttery leather messenger-like bag, bordering on a satchel, a miniature leather hold-all. How small the stitches were! Minute! Embroidered in crimson on the front, the word:

CAPACIOUS.

I turned it over and found the words—'any thing, solemn, slight or beautiful.'

I knew immediately this was a purse dedicated to Virginia Woolf. When I had first learned of Ingrid-Simone's penchant for purses, I had brought in Woolf's diary and read out loud in my best fake British accent for her the famous line, "What sort of diary should I like mine to be? Something loose knit and yet not slovenly, so elastic that it will embrace any thing, solemn, slight or beautiful that comes into my mind. I should like it to resemble some deep old desk, or capacious hold-all, in which one flings a mass of odds and ends without looking them through."

While I was drinking in the contents of the tiny box, turning the purse over in my hand, Ingrid-Simone recited these lines from Woolf. Then, just as she was saying, in a much better British accent than I managed, —you must see the flinging, the flinging, you must look them through, my love, I noticed her embroidered signature below the word capacious: I.s. In crimson and unmistakable, however infinitesimal.

I opened the clasp, feeling like Alice in Wonderland when she had grown very tall. Instantly I imagined the conditions in which this little work of art had been made. I imagined Ingrid-Simone's apartment—I knew that much, that she lived in an apartment. Once she told me that she had hung swaths of fabric everywhere. To walk into the kitchen you had to walk through layers of Indian silk in pinks, yellows and oranges, some with gold sequins.

She took the purse from me then, I was taking too long. —Hold out your hand, she said, and I did, smiling what was probably a drunken smile, hoping that no one would come into the store and ruin the moment. Later I found out that she had locked the front door. —Who cares, she said, —if someone can't come in and browse, run their hands over the rows of jackets and pants as a child would run a stick along the rungs of a metal fence. She was not afraid of being caught out, though I admit, it made me feel uneasy when I found out.

In the palm of my hand fit, all in miniature:

> a letter complete with postage stamp, addressed to Vita Sackville-West.
> a netting filled with heart-shaped stones, which were, in fact, heart shaped candies, whittled down and painted
> a white flower
> a cigarette in its holder.
> a moth
> a copy of *Ulysses*
> magazine clippings
> a portrait of Virginia Woolf done by Vanessa
> a pencil, the one she had bought while street-haunting
> five hundred pounds
> a candle stub
> a diary, bound in boards to the proper specifications—the cover being a marbled Florentine paper.

She handed me a magnifying glass, about the size of my eye. I opened the diary, and within I found several quotations about the soul transcribed from Woolf's diary which, squinting, I slowly read aloud, Ingrid-Simone mouthing the same words as though she couldn't help herself from doing so.

"As for the soul; why did I say I would leave it out? I forget. And the truth is, one can't write directly about the soul. Looked at, it vanishes."

"But oh the delicacy and complexity of the soul—for haven't I begun to tap her and listen to her breathing after all?"

"I want to give the slipperiness of the soul. I have been too tolerant too often. The truth is people scarcely care for each other. They have this insane instinct for life. But they never become attached to anything outside themselves."

I later underlined these quotations in my copy of Woolf's diaries. But at that moment, I was overwhelmed. And also uncomfortable. This gift was so personal and a very large part of me liked to keep my distance from people. Why was that? Oh sure, I had been burned by this friend or that, who hadn't? Nothing out of the ordinary, nothing that had caused me to quite lose faith in humankind, nothing so drastic, though I had really given up on the idea of friendship and felt I was growing too old for kindred spirits. I sensed, perhaps, that I meant more to her than I thought she could mean to me. I was born wary. I just was. And whenever I talked myself out of that wariness on the grounds that it was plainly foolish, I got burned. I got sent a flaming email or found myself backing away, slowly, carefully, having discovered something unsavoury. I had spent far too much time analysing the nature of women's friendships when I should have been doing something productive, like looking for a decent way to make a living that didn't ravage the soul, as this job would do without the fine company of Ingrid-Simone.

Like Woolf, I had an insane instinct for life. I couldn't become too attached to anything outside of myself. But when someone gives you a gift like this...well, it blew my mind. The craftsmanship, the time that went into making it, the talent, and the generosity of spirit were extraordinary. And when I said this, she replied, —Oh, yes... my very obscure talent, not too difficult to be generous with that then, is it? And smiled her becalming smile, downplaying the whole thing, laughing at herself. And then, more seriously, she said, —what I've tried to do is to put the breath of her soul, the delicacy, the complexity, in that street-haunting bag. And, hmm. I don't know if I've done that, but I've tried, I tried to feel it, to breathe a certain way when I made it. When I designed it. I tried to put the quest for the pencil into that bag. The deep walking breath of a woman such as Woolf. Or maybe Mrs. Dalloway. The sort of even and hearty and yet delicate breath of a woman who goes questing for a pencil at night, or stops to buy her own flowers, the insane harmony of that. Do you know it's true, people scarcely care for each other, but it doesn't have to be that way, does it?

—Now. Just put it away, take it. Don't think about. Hmm? It was just one of those ideas I had, and I couldn't stop until it was finished or meant something and I thought it might to you.

So, I put it away and she unlocked the front door and suddenly the store was full of customers asking for this or that, saying they had an occasion for which they needed a dress immediately, and the dressing rooms were full, the cash register busy, and we scurried around after people, finding sizes and hanging up discards. Me, intermittently watching Ingrid-Simone very kindly directing a woman with frighteningly pulled back facial skin and protruding backbones away from the feathered gowns and toward a soft grey flowing number. I admired this, since I was too tired to care so much. Not that I wanted people to leave the store with something they looked terrible in, but I lacked the ability to direct them, to manoeuvre them toward what might flatter. Instead, I rang in purchases and helped ladies find sizes, colours, skirts and jackets. Ingrid-Simone was the creative one, adding things to dressing rooms, draping a scarf over the arm of a woman holding a green dress, pointing out a matching purse or mentioning a sash or belt that would enhance the garment. This went on until closing time.

c/ɔ

What a beautiful thing, this gift. I took it home and sat for a long time in my turquoise chair before taking off my tall boots. I took up the pen I had left on the wobbly side table and retrieved the notebook I had in my handbag. I set the box on the table and began to write and write. The next day I repeated some of what I wrote to Ingrid-Simone. A condensed version, less fragmented. I was afraid. I wrote that down on one page.

Why was I afraid? I thought about past friendships. I thought about what Derrida said in his book *Politics of Friendship*. A book I had bought on a whim, trying to feel intelligent during a certain emotionally crushing break-up with a fellow grad student friend, which is perhaps an entirely unique category of friendship. Left on my shelf for years and never read, I only took it down when I began working at Theodora's. I found it sitting on the table by the door, the table that looked similar to the one Jane Austen had written on. I picked it up and thumbed through, reading the bits I had underlined. "The two concepts (friend/enemy) consequently intersect and ceaselessly change places." Is this true I wondered?

I had vowed to give up on friendship. I had. What precipitated this, in short, was that the last several close friendships I had had with women had gone miserably wrong, though I do not exactly think of them as enemies now. Each went odd, askew for a different reason. One of them because my idea of a close friendship was rather more Georgic—I had wanted to write letters and be close in the manner of Jane Austen and her sister Cassandra. And she had wanted the relationship to be more Sapphic. I could not try things on for the sake of it or because it was fashionable. I had felt it would diminish my friend, were I to merely pretend interest in caressing her, in being caressed by her.

Another woman I thought I was close to wrote me a flaming email that seemed to come from nowhere. Obviously she had been fuming about me for ages and I foolishly had been utterly dumb to it. I was too opinionated; I didn't appreciate her enough or cheer her on properly. I questioned her activities, as I might call into question a situation in a literary text. Maybe we were too much the same and maybe I should have spent more time analysing my faults or my shortcomings but my immediate reaction was just to run. To avoid. To stay as far away as I could from this person. Which was difficult at a small university.

I didn't leave the university because of her. I left in truth because I could not, did not want, to overcome my extreme shyness. As part of the program, I needed to teach a class. I wouldn't always be able to hide behind research assistantships or the copy-editing of obscure scholarly periodicals. As a professor, I would be constantly teaching classes. I knew this going in. And I knew that it would destroy me. I had barely managed to attend a class, participate in it, without crumbling. Mainly I had sat at whatever conference table I found myself and tried to assume an expression of intelligence. I had volunteered small opinions when I could but even the most miniscule threat of being called upon froze my brain, which of course made it all worse. When called on, I had mumbled, blank and stupid. How could I formulate thoughts, when my brain was in a panic state?

When all eyes around the table made their way to me, I could feel myself burning. My palms were clammy. But maybe what went on internally was more interesting. I felt as though I had been boiled down to an essential truth. An internal dialogue, impossible to examine, ensued: Can't. Must. Say something. Deflect. Turn your answer into a question. Lips won't move.

Heart beating. Say something you wrote down in your notes, unconnected. Try to connect it. Stop the redness, breathe. More redness instead. Very warm. Look, the person across from me has violet eyes, actually violet. The question. Directed at me. What was it? They're all looking. I appeared deep in thought until now. Uncomfortable. Any longer and they will know. They will know. I've lost what we were discussing. Change the subject. Keep it short. Ask another student something, relate it to what they said, so they can pick up the thread. Bail me out. Might faint.

A white light always arrived and saturated the mind. So that looking out, there was a blindness, a holiness that I wanted to go into, to delve deeper into, but instead, the rules of society forced me to attempt to swim, damp-feathered, against the light's brilliant current.

Being put on the spot and failing to express myself was made worse by the after-tremors. The inward kicking of self. The shrinking, the cringing. This was not something easily expunged. At home alone, lying in bed, a moan would escape. A phrase I had uttered, a thought that had escaped me, would arrive in my mind, a phantom, haunting me, and I would respond involuntarily with a deep, low moan that I wouldn't always recognize as my own. Sometimes I needed to rock myself back and forth, a babe, swaddle myself and breathe, until the moment when I could return to my childhood.

Aspects of my shyness tormented me. And yet I did not give it up. I thought shyness allowed me to look at flowers more closely, spring grass, and the light that rested on leaves illuminating their delicate veins. I was sensitive to the way snow fell, the rate of it, the shape of the flakes, I could feel it under my skin, falling into the cold parts of me, into the warm. I understood snow melting onto spring grass utterly and completely. A patient form of madness, shyness is, and I wanted to live it as one lives certain flowers, the hibiscus for example.

I told Ingrid-Simone about my shyness and she said, —I think I completely understand. I told her how I thought it was fated that I would end up working at Theodora's. I felt there was something pre-ordained about it. I told her about my mother, who was extremely agoraphobic. Which didn't really have much to do with shyness on her part but maybe did for me. Mostly I negligently communicated with my mother via snail mail. Letters. I tried to write her long, beautiful letters. I chose stamps with flowers on them at the post office. I embellished with movie stubs, candy bar wrappers, dried flowers. I enclosed small packets of spice. Miniature envelopes filled with pollen, sand, threads of saffron. We both pretended it was normal to want to stay indoors. To order groceries online.

Sometimes I mailed the letters, sometimes I went to her door and knocked. The doorbell startled her so badly. I knocked and knocked and then waited. Could feel her looking out windows. I stood back so she could see it was me, pretending that I couldn't feel her eyes. Usually she let me in and we sat at the kitchen table and drank tea. Other times she couldn't face it. Opening the door, I suppose. Me. Or maybe it wasn't me. I never took it personally. When she opened the door to someone, the rest of the universe came in too. And all of the dark and secret spaces within that person entered as well. The fears that made someone keep secrets. And she had enough fears of her own.

On one of my recent visits, I told my mother that as a child I was torn between two fantasies. I wanted to fly, and as I walked home from lunch, I would look up and see a seagull, and imagine that I was that bird. I flew those five blocks home in my mind's eye, I soared, cutting through the air cleanly, on my glossy and pristine white wings, and would always be mildly surprised when she asked me why it took me so long. It had seemed to go by so quickly.

But the other childhood fantasy I had was that I could disappear. That I could blink my eyes a certain way and disappear from sight. Then, in school, when the teacher started asking questions, casting an eye about, I could just blink. First I would become luminous and then there would be that same feeling, as if disappearing into flight. I would be sitting in a place of silence; I could close my eyes and be the milky quiet. And maybe when I was dreaming up this scenario I enacted my own disappearance, for who could see me in my daydreams, alone? How liberating it was, how comforting, to drift into an inner quiet, sinking down into one's self, one's truest most liquid self, so that all through life it was possible to return to this milky embrace, to be saved by it, to have recourse to it, floating for a while, remembering without words, without warbling, this possibility of being unencumbered and un-infringed upon. So that, emerging, I always felt as if I were on the verge of inventing something wonderful, like self-propelled flight or the most marvellous flavour of candy, or being the first to discover a certain delicious slant of light, another realm.

The strange thing about having tea with my mother was, once you were in, once you crossed the threshold, all seemed normal. She lived a completely normal existence in one way. Her house was clean and orderly but not obsessively so. It was comfortable. We sat at her kitchen table and drank Red Rose tea and she put out a couple of cookies that she baked, usually something pretending to be healthy, oatmeal raisin or pumpkin spice. When I asked if she had everything she needed, or if I could bring her anything next time, she always laughed and waved her hand. —Oh no, everything comes to me these days, so simple, she said. —I can get anything, food, clothes, magazines, books, all on the internet. And she always dressed nicely, plainly, but nice. Her clothes fit well. She wore shoes in the house. They showed some sign of wear but were always perfectly clean, like the gym shoes you have in elementary school.

৩

We really began telling each other things about ourselves, Ingrid-Simone Stephens and I, after she gave me Woolf's purse. Small divulgences that added up. Tesserae in a mosaic. It all happened there in the store, our relationship. Which seemed odd in a way, though I had done the same with friends at the university too. Never inviting anyone into my apartment, my home.

—Oh, I just pretend to be sweet, I'm not at all. I'm really quite unscrupulous.

She said things like this with a sly look and a laugh over her shoulder and walked quickly away. I found it immensely amusing when she said such things. I only saw rather magical evidence to the contrary. I thought I should be more patient and sweet with the customers, like she was, and told her so. Customers adored her and she was often getting compliments. Sometimes Florine even shared an email she got from one of them in praise of Ingrid-Simone. Certainly this never happened to me.

Ingrid-Simone told me she was always tracking the stars that appeared in movie adaptations of Jane Austen novels. —I care about them, she said. —I know it sounds more like I'm stalking them or have celebrity crushes on them, which naturally I do. And here she winked at me, laughing at herself, such an infectious laugh, pure music. —But you know, she said, I wonder about what happens after you've played Mr. Knightley or Mr. Darcy or Edmund or dear Wentworth or silly Edward Ferrars. So yes, I do like to take care of them, in my mind, I know it's only in my mind. I want to make sure they're content and serene. And I want to see if they go on being anything like the characters they portrayed. She took out several butter-pat notebooks from her bosom and began flipping through them as one would thumb through a flip-book. I could barely make out her usual small handwriting. —And I keep lists on them, she said, —see, Ciaran Hinds, Colin Firth, Jeremy Northam, Hugh Grant, Jonny Lee Miller, especially him. Really, I'd like to make a movie with just them and scratch the heroines, you know? A movie about their lives after Austen, a documentary.

And here she laughed loudly; I had never heard this particularly deep but giddy laugh from her. —I'm joking of course, she said. —But I read the books when I was just a kid in high school, we didn't have a TV and I couldn't afford to go to movies, hadn't even heard of the BBC. I didn't really know there were movies until much later. But I sat in the library and read Austen. All one summer. I lived at Hartfield and Pemberley. In humble cottages and glorious estates. I walked through mud to meet my sister. All that summer I was rescued and I feel I owe a massive debt to those who rescued me. Jane Austen, above all. But since I was the heroine, completely and naively so, I am quite in service to these characters. When I discovered the movies and watched them over and over I became oddly thankful to the actors portraying those gentlemen who made that one particular summer bearable, that summer when I became so obsessed with Elizabeth and Emma and Fanny and Anne and Elinor. I talked like them, in my head, had conversations in their voices with myself, I talked to all the gentlemen, asking their advice, and then I even began talking to the movie renditions, because they were closer somehow. Tried to talk myself sane you see. I was quite miserable and quite ready to leave this life, I'm not kidding.

—You know I've worried about them. As human beings. Whether a tattoo was a good idea, whether they are kind enough to their wives, though I'm sure they are, I hope they are. Whether they will be forgotten, or ignored, or if they will be swarmed by paparazzi, or if they're offered decent roles. I know, it's idiotic, but I find myself hoping for them. For their fulfilment.

—Someone, you see, before my Austen mania, gave me a copy of *Tess of the D'Urbervilles*. It overwhelmed me. I identified with Tess. I was Tess. I am. And I hated her for making me feel her sorrow and helplessness and for not explaining things properly to Angel Clare at the proper moments. And she named her baby Sorrow, which I will never forgive her for, never. Sorrow! Intolerable. The book ruined me, I'm not exaggerating; I had a nervous breakdown over this book, hovering over it as I did.

—So you can see why it was necessary to escape. And why I had conversations with Jonny Lee Miller in my head. I suppose I picked him because he'd been both Edmund and Knightley. Both characters were excellent at passing out advice. Then I read that he was in a TV show where he played a lawyer for whom George Michael appeared and sang, "you've got to have faith." It's not as though I ever wrote him fan mail, other than in my head, because I'm not the sort to infringe on real lives with my fantasy one, you know, and I wouldn't want to embarrass him. I imagine I would be an embarrassment to him, would seem quite odd! Hmm.

The truth was I couldn't see why it was necessary for her to escape. I mean, I thought I could at the time, we all needed to escape a bit, but it was a lot to take in at that moment—her earnestness, her sweetness, her very real concern, the endearing way she expressed herself, the interesting way she punctuated her sentences, drawing out this word and that one, and then punching up another. And of course part of me was just delighted by the description, by the anecdotal evidence, of this reader response that is often difficult or impossible to record in the university environment, since everyone wants to appear intelligent and would never admit to adoring vintage Harlequin romances and certainly not to holding conversations with fictional characters or worrying about the altogether too-handsome actors that played them. This all seemed very real to me. While Ingrid-Simone spoke, I recalled all those many breaks my colleagues and I had taken at the midway point in grad classes, outside the temperature-controlled Special Collections room, swooning under the worn marble staircase, leaning against the maple wood walls, where we talked about marginalia and how to decipher the early modern manuscript, and about access to print at a juncture of time when the manuscript was just as prevalent and more highly thought of than the printed word. And we talked about the circulation of commonplace books and what a beautiful process that must have been, copying out a poem and then passing it along to another to copy in their own commonplace book, and how words got transposed or changed or revised along the way, by accident or by intention. We drank our coffees and Diet Cokes and discussed Colin Firth. And laughed at how we had gone from talking of the ways in which post-structuralist thought could apply to 17th century polemical texts by women to discussing the merits of a movie star's physique, the gloriousness of his accent, his ability to smoulder and in short, all his captivating charms.

The first bits I recorded in a notebook that evening were: Jane Austen as an antidote for Thomas Hardy, and, interaction with fictional characters off the page, and, Austen as a balm for life, and, a note to myself, research strong reader response to *Tess of the D'Urbervilles*. I made a note to look up Jonny Lee Miller. I had down the word: tattoo, the word: sorrow. I scrawled down: faith. I noted such things as what Ingrid-Simone was wearing: high black boots with a moderate but showy heel, a pencil skirt, red tights, red shirt with tattoo-like design emblazoned on the front but obscured by a flowing dark grey ruffled, almost Victorian, sweater. I noted: sweet but unscrupulous, and then wrote: hardly unscrupulous after it and underlined the word 'hardly.' I fantasized about going back to grad school and writing a dissertation about reader-response, about romance, about a particular un-named reader.

She also talked about an extravagantly horrible dream she had on numerous occasions, which caused her to cease watching cooking shows before bed. She dreamed one of the gentlemen, sometimes Mr. Darcy (Colin Firth), more often Mr. Knightley (Jonny Lee Miller), rang her doorbell wearing forest green velvet tailcoats and riding boots, calling for dinner. And she was expected to make something out of the ingredients that she found magically in her kitchen. —The thing is, she said, —I don't cook, hardly. Well, I do make excellent poached eggs. But am I to offer Mr. Knightley poached eggs and a Diet Coke? I'm in misery. It's the worst possible dream. Besides, I don't want to meet them, I can't meet them. I know I'm ridiculous and my fantasy would be utterly ruined if I were to actually meet them! It's a nightmare, not a dream; it's a bizarre nightmare. I'm given scallops and told to pan sear them and assemble a watermelon salsa. I just can't do that. I only have one pan for heaven's sake. I only have two plates that I picked up at Value Village and one set of cutlery. Could I ask them to share?

—What did you do, I asked?

—Oh, the only thing I could do, I panicked so bloody much that finally I woke up!

And here she laughed her sparkly etude and I thought of Chopin and white twinkle lights on late summer nights and sequins at a dull office party.

❧

Winter was all around. I want to keep reminding myself of that. The cold was like waves, coming to shore and retreating. Everywhere white nothingness. But how real. The air was biting and inhospitable at times but at others, bracing and enlivening. Brisk, quiet. There was time and space to be present to the beauty of snowfalls, so unpredictable. The store, too, seemed to breathe differently in winter. When the front door opened to let someone in, the store gulped in the winter air and when they left, it expelled. In the moment of the whoosh of air, sometimes I would hear the song of a winter bird and later I would approach the air and scratch bird tracks into the patterns of frost on the window beside the door.

❧

I'm not sure when she told me about her tattoo. I have tried to keep my notebook entries and sticky notes, the serviettes, bus passes, and bills, all in some semblance of order. But sometimes one slips out of the elastic bands I wrapped them in or I find it later in a jacket pocket, written while walking and therefore difficult to read. I've never been able to write legibly while walking. There's no class or booklet that teaches a person such a useful skill.

I caught a glimpse of the tattoo, actually. A word: "overdo." I don't think she was trying to conceal it, but as it was on her left shoulder and since it was winter, she had been wearing a multitude of layers, lots of sweaters and scarves. But that day she had a shirt with a V at the back, and as she was reaching for something, I caught a glimpse. Everyone had a tattoo those days, except me I'm sure, so it was not such a big deal. But I was curious as to what it is. A purse—a small red purse, with a 1950s feeling to it. Circled around it in a delicate script, with the word 'overdo'at the top of the circle, as an injunction or instigation—

"Do not overdo the bag, Winnie,"

from Beckett's play, *Happy Days.* It was relatively new, then, as I know she had only discovered the play not long after we met. And maybe that surprised me most. That she hadn't murmured a word of it. Not that I expected her to tell me everything, and when I mentioned it, she was completely open about it. Pulled her shirt down over her shoulder so I could get a better look.

—Oh, Shaya, the pain was unbearable! But I hummed through the procedure, which helped. It was worth it, though, to have that very moment in the play so close to me.

—I had to go back to get the purse inked in red. And oh I know one day I'll feel foolish and regret it horribly and go have it removed at great expense and considerable pain. Right now though, it makes me feel quite splendid and hopeful.

She told me all of this when I mentioned the tattoo, so I don't know why I went around feeling hurt that whole day. But I did.

❧

How do we get to know someone then? So much clouds our approach to one another, obfuscates the light that would ease through a window and engulf the two souls standing beside the sill. I thought about happiness, and how the degree to which we feel happy impinges upon our interactions, how intently we listen to another, how we interpret the gestures a friend makes in our presence. How our recent triumphs and infirmities come into play. And I was not particularly content; I was not at peace. I had even sunk to feeling I never could feel peace, would never quite be happy.

Why did I so desperately want to get to know her? I see now that this was one of my goals, though I wouldn't have put it so at the time. I had studied English literature for eight years, continually asking myself how authors create convincing characters, how is it that they make us understand more about ourselves as we come to understand a fictional character? There had been a length of time when I came at these questions more esoterically, through a veil of theory, which of course has its uses. What secrets does the text hold for the reader willing to make creative and wild connections? I was interested in the revelation of character by observing the language they used and the words used to describe them. I monitored the action and admired the scenes where I gained more insight about them. What did the presence of a lamp in a drawing room signify when placed near the hero, for example? I prided myself on missing nothing, on understanding. I excavated the author's original manuscripts and searched their marginalia, the edits they had made, earlier versions of their text. I noted where changes had occurred, been built upon. But this pertained best to fiction and when I kept trying to translate my rather menial existence as shopgirl, using these esoteric tools I had acquired in academe, well, I'm not sure I managed terribly well.

☙

On a day off, especially if it were particularly cold out and snowing, I stayed in my bachelor apartment, wrapped myself in a blanket and laid down on my chaise longue. I had only the turquoise chair by the door and the scrolled chaise and that was all besides my futon, which was in the area behind the Band-Aid coloured plastic screen. The screen fit into metal grooves and could be shoved into a compartment in the wall to make the space appear larger, but I always left the screen unfurled, open. I didn't want to see my unmade bed, the white duvet, the white Egyptian cotton sheets, the long white voluminous nightgown that I dropped in the centre. Too tempting. I knew I, Shaya Neige, could live there, in my bed white as snow, staring at the seafoam blue walls, that I would never want to leave, would rather wander around all day in my bachelor apartment, dancing and spinning, in my nightgown that was like a skin, I knew it so well. Pretending I was free, as angels must feel in their infinite levitation. Collapsing onto my bed and relinquishing myself to the wonderful, soft and pleasing energy of dreams.

I forced myself to rise, and dress, and comb my hair and put on lip gloss. I ate my bowl of cereal on the rough, red velvet chaise longue, which I had claimed from a sketchy back alley when I first moved out. One of the legs had broken off, and I had stacked five or six novels to replace it. I read this book, and that one. I scribbled notes in my notebook. I often wrote about Ingrid-Simone. I jotted down random things she told me before I forgot them. Not for the purposes of making up a story about her but because recording them seemed important. She had her toast and tea in the bathtub while reading a novel every morning because it not only saved time but she liked the feeling of being simultaneously efficient and self-indulgent. She liked the way paper lunch bags felt, the coarse exterior, the waxy interior, and used them to carry everything. Books, sandwiches, loose change. She kept one folded in her coat pocket nearly all the time. And she loved sandwiches. —The one thing I'm really good at, she said, —is making sandwiches. I hardly ever make them though because they require too many ingredients to have on hand all at once. I like them because they're cold and layered and never just one thing.

Today I let her look at the contents of my purse.

I wrote this on a sticky note, a pale yellow one, the ordinary kind. I didn't date the note. But when I read, "today I let her look at the contents of my purse," I was there. After that line, I scrawled: Stein, I scribbled: Freud. I probably said to Ingrid-Simone, —there's a bit by Gertrude Stein in *Tender Buttons*, but I cannot recall if I did. I might have said, —oh, just think what Freud would say about this, and winked.

Stein said, "A purse was not green, it was not straw colour, it was hardly seen and it had a use a long use and the chain, the chain was never missing, it was not misplaced, it showed that it was open, that is all that it showed."

Later I received a miniature green Stein purse proclaiming that it was not green or made of straw and it had a long chain and was lodged open.

There was an openness between us but also the understanding that we didn't need to reveal all. For there must have been a pocket or a concealed and zippered section of my purse that was not divulged. Perhaps it was the pocket that held a pad of sticky notes, random scraps of scrawled upon paper. I hid these from her. Which seemed reasonable.

Was it strange that I should have been writing a dissertation, had abandoned it, to write random jottings in purse-sized notebooks and on myriad pale sticky notes about a young woman I barely knew? But it seemed real to me. What is that line from Rilke about his friend, Lou Andreas-Salome, "you alone are real to me?" All that winter, she was, Ingrid-Simone, my young friend who in some ways was a mirror of my younger self, a self that I couldn't have been but dreamed about even so. The dissertation didn't choose me, but this other method of writing did.

I think now that she expected that I would say no. I could never ask to look inside anyone's purse. Maybe this was a generational thing. I wanted to say no, the word no was in my head, but the thought of slighting her was unbearable.

—Do you know there are people who believe that the contents of a purse reveal the soul of the one who carries it? I asked her.

—Oh, yes, I know I know, she said, with that devilish gleam in her eyes that was always delightful to witness, because of her ridiculous sweetness.

—You will find my soul to be rather dull, I'm afraid, said I.

What was in my purse that day? The usual conglomeration of softly worn, wafered notebooks, light blue lined post-its, a few of the yellow ones too. These rattled around in the open, the ordinary blank ones. Once I wrote on them, I stuffed them into the side compartment where they emitted a glow. My Covergirl compact, Revlon lipstick number 002, pink pout. Detritus.

Usually I carried a candy bar, a coconut one. There were long, narrow packets of Starbucks' instant coffee because I had read that Clarice Lispector mixed coffee with Coca-Cola when she needed to be extremely awake, though I might be misrepresenting this because I can no longer find the passage. I kept the packets of coffee to pour into my cans of pop that I sometimes brought in my lunch. There was a cocktail napkin from a wedding I had been to that had the names of the bride and groom, the date of their ceremony, and the implausible words "eloquence, sublime, Rumi" scrawled on it. Ingrid-Simone looked at this and laughed, but said no more.

She was arrested by a copy of Simone Weil's *Waiting for God*, which seems to me now to be a strange coincidence, an eerie one, but then it seemed utterly reasonable, inevitable, a coherent piece in the puzzle that was our lives. Before then, I had never noticed, never connected their names, maybe because Simone Weil was for me, simoneweil, and Ingrid-Simone was always ingridsimone.

She extracted *Waiting for God* from what I came to think of as my soul-spill. There was a feather I had found when I left the building that housed the English Department, fleeing the person who I was not. Blurrily, I had noticed, a peripheral glance, a feather calling to me from the grass beside the sidewalk. It must have fluttered a little. I had hardly slowed down as to pick it up and continue. I had broken into a run, my hand outstretched, be-feathered, Daphne-like, for a few short steps before resuming my self-conscious, poised gait.

Feathers followed me, I later learned. But then, Ingrid-Simone plucked this feather from my belongings, from amid the dollar coins, the Trident gum and the Bounty chocolate wrappers. She held it in her hand, twirled it, fluttered it along her chin as she perused. When she saw the book, she immediately set down the feather. —Simone! She said. A small post-it note had become affixed to the cover on which I had written, "What are you going through?" page 115. Which is where she flipped to directly upon reading my cramped and unusual script—half writing, half printing.

I had put dark brackets around the paragraph that began, "The love of our neighbour in all its fullness simply means being able to say to him: 'What are you going through?'" Weil was talking about the Grail quest, about the king afflicted with a terrible wound, experiencing excruciating pain. She was talking about suffering. The Grail was said to belong to the one who is compelled, feels the compassion, knows to ask, and, most importantly, has the courage to ask the king, "What are you going through?" Which seemed a very easy thing to do, but of course this is complicated by those cold and sometimes necessary distances we keep from one another as human beings, by our reservations, by our worries about what might be appropriate, by protocols, by hesitation, by over-interpretation of who the sorrowing suffering Grail king might truly be.

How is one to do this? I had underlined this sentence and circled the word soul and that is what Ingrid-Simone read aloud, —"The soul empties itself of all its own contents in order to receive into itself the being it is looking at, just as he is, in all his truth."

—But how difficult to empty one's soul! She knew this immediately. And then she made the connection between the emptying of the purse and the emptying of the soul, and her name, in part, on the book.

—It seems a message, a darling message. We could call the message, Sorrow. But we won't, she said with a lopsided smile. —No, we won't. I refuse.

And still I did not ask her at that moment, "What are you going through?"

I did not ask.

Later I found myself thinking deeply on this subject—how one can feel compassion and not act on it, not voice it.

We put the contents back into the purse. She took my mangled feather and placed it as a marker on page 115. I wedged the book back into my handbag, along with the matte pink tube of lipstick and sugarless chewing gum.

The Red Handbag

That winter of the record lows, of frozen cheeks and sugar frosted hair, I put less milk in my coffee. Was I becoming more bitter? Or was it that I had less of a need for what is mellow and milky.

The first day we decided to follow Florine home, so we might at least know where she lived, it snowed. We were not yet oppressed by the early darkness as we would be later in the winter. The snow was illuminated by the streetlights and the first large flakes seemed like ethereal fireflies, spinning floating aloft. We left the store by the front door and Florine locked us out. She then exited from the rear of the building. We stood outside the store as we often did, before setting off in opposite directions. Pulling our scarves up, and our hats down.

But this night we waited before wordlessly skirting around the building. It was childish but we were utterly serious. It seemed a simple idea, to spy her around the building's edge, to see what direction she went and to follow her footsteps in the snow. We hadn't expected that first night for Florine to head down into the ravine at the end of the first block, into the trees, down a steep path. She had seen us, felt us, she had felt followed, we surmised, and so we held back. But on other numerous occasions when we had the inkling to follow her, she always headed down into the ravine, always at a different spot so that no path was worn.

Once we dashed down the steep incline, sliding and grasping at small trees for balance, to a paved footpath, over the pedestrian bridge, and back onto sidewalks. Down the block with old clapboard houses, some refurbished, some dilapidated. Followed by a couple of blocks of tall apartment buildings with blue-black windows. We thought we had caught up to Florine; we slowed. For several more blocks we followed a woman with a long black coat, carrying a huge satchel. Ingrid-Simone said, —no, stop. It's not her. We hurried then and caught up and it was not Florine.

—How did you know, I asked.

Ingrid-Simone said, —the music I heard wasn't right. It should have been more Gorecki, *Symphony of Sorrowful Songs.* And what I was getting was more, hmmmmm, a waltz, Strauss, *The Voices of Spring.* Poor Florine, we both nodded.

We became much better at identifying her. All that winter, we caught glimpses of her but never learned where she lived, or very much about her at all. Once, I looked out of my apartment window at 3am and I was sure I saw her walking by, street-haunting, Woolfian, going to buy a pencil, I imagined. Hunched over, looking at the cold cement, it must not have mattered to her where she was, just that she was moving. Another time, Ingrid-Simone reported seeing her pedalling her blue bicycle with such large wheels in the middle of the night, down sidewalks, slow—dream-slow. She rubbed her eyes and shook her head and Florine was still riding, teetering along.

—I was worried, said Ingrid-Simone —because it was a cold night, and I could see a fog around her, her breath, but she was only wearing a sweater, a big wool one, navy blue, but still, only a sweater.

—Perhaps she had many layers, I offered.

—Yes, Ingrid-Simone said, —she is a many layered woman, and she laughed, her musical laugh.

Back at the store, Florine seemed no worse for the wear.

We worried about not worrying about Florine, some days. We were so absorbed by reading the narrow confines of our lives and by making it interesting in myriad ways, in ways that scarcely seem so now. In the end, what did we learn of Florine that winter? Almost nothing. We learned, I suppose, how to keep company with her silence, to listen to the rhythm of her footsteps, to recognize how she walked from great and dim distances: slightly stooped, her walk lilting and graceful in the manner of say, an ostrich that believed in its own flight. We knew her pace, her gait. Could identify her silhouette on cement walls and through café windows. We learned how to keep watch. How not to get caught. Or did she know? We learned how to leave be. Though following her felt a bit like a game, we truly were respectful of her. We thought a great deal about the space between us. We learned to imagine and not know, to try to understand without knowing, to ask small questions, to listen. Ingrid-Simone could do an imitation of the way Florine breathed, the rhythm of it, the slight catch every so many breaths, the nervous sniffs, the long sighs, and the way she puffed out every so often, the way a horse will breathe out over a carrot in an outstretched hand.

We imagined the possibility that she had no home. That she walked out away from the store at closing time and came back much later. That she slept in the office chair, tipped back, her feet on the desk. That she kept her clothes in the filing cabinet and her toothbrush in the desk drawer.

We talked some days, low and quiet, when the store was empty or nearly so, about those things we cannot usually ask others. We didn't feel we could ask Florine where she lived, or what she loved, or who she was. There were the things we felt about her, hardly knowing her. We could list these. There was a deep sorrow in her, she was so fragile and she must have led a radically different life from the one she was in at that moment. Ingrid-Simone heard her soul music, she said. It went with the auras of people often, but not always.

—Fernando Pessoa, Ingrid-Simone said, —once wrote "My soul is a secret orchestra, but I don't know what instruments—strings, harps, cymbals, drums—strum and bang inside me. I only know myself as the symphony." But I believe we can also at times hear the secret orchestra in another. And as for me, I don't know that my soul is not a symphony, because sometimes I hear it being plucked, at other times I surely hear flute music, so many wind instruments. There are, at times, the solitary bleatings of an oboe. I'm certain of it. Hmmmmm. I must be composed of awkward soloists with stage fright!

—But what I need to know is when the soul's music begins. At birth, do you think it's at birth? And can you absorb the soul music of someone when they die? What happens to it do you think? And then, there's the question of pre-existence, the bluebird of happiness, you know, the old Technicolor movie with Shirley Temple. All the little angelic souls waiting to be born. Some of them so wise. Is the soul born and then once it leaves the body in death, does it get to be re-born again, stand in queue? And then, what inhabits the soul? Remember the line from Emily Dickinson? "Hope is the thing with feathers / that perches in the soul." I imagine sometimes that the soul is a tree, with all these branches, perches, you know.

—Oh, I know philosophers have pondered this for hundreds of years, the state of the soul before and after death, the question of whether or not the mother shares the baby's soul while it's in utero, but I can't stop thinking about it. What is the soul? I cannot stop asking. What is the soul?

The Rumi lines were a sort of nervous twitch for her at times, an incantation, a mantra, said under her breath, and if you didn't know the lines, it would have been possible to miss them entirely. Not knowing Ingrid-Simone, you might mistake these mutterings for a pop song, hummed absentmindedly.

Early on I realized that Ingrid-Simone was profoundly more intelligent than I am, though she was young and I was the one who had spent a decade in university. Soon, I hardly blinked when she dropped someone like Fernando Pessoa into the conversation and continued with a mash-up of poetry and film references, and then proceeded to mull over a position, philosophically and poetically. She felt free, I flattered myself, to talk to me in this manner because she knew I would understand. Where before I reeled with the types of things she thought about and knew and could memorize, I had learned to be quiet and listen and gently question, though of course more often than not we were interrupted.

The bell on the door would jangle and she would jump off the front desk and we would resume our tasks, helping the customers find this or that and so on.

We spent a great deal of time reading the people who come into the store. A game we developed together, I suppose. A woman in her fifties left the store and we tossed words back and forth:

—Caesar salad.

—Liquid lunch, Ingrid Simone countered.

—Divorcee, I interjected —Charitable organization. Executive.

—Kind, Ingrid-Simone said softly, then with sadness, —Pushover.

A girl in her twenties entered.

—Shallow, I said.

—Troubled, angry, Ingrid-Simone responded. —Convinced she is right.

And then, one of us would ask, —are you certain?

No, no we never were.

Even amid all our glorious discussions, often so unconnected and breezy, and then intense and insistent, I sensed that Ingrid-Simone was learning to become ruthlessly lonely.

I want to tell you more about her, all the little things that were so delightful. I wanted to record them as a tired mother with her newborn begins to record beautifully incoherent snippets of behaviour, divine to her, sacred. When and where a first step was taken, surprising phrases, moments that reveal how a person has been formed, has come into themselves. I wanted to write down all the lovely bits that were Ingrid-Simone before I tell you about her unravelling. I don't want to misuse what I have been given. I wanted to watch over her, to let my watching over her change me. To record, also, those alterations in me. Did we change each other? I only know she changed me.

Florine rolled out a rack of clothes, letting it fly. —Not much today, she said, with an unlit cigarette hanging from her lip as the metal rack reverberated. That music. She must have forgotten it was there. I mean the cigarette. And on the front counter she dumped a rather huge sagging cardboard box full of a heap of jumbled pumps, necklaces and purses. One of the necklaces hung over the edge, a piece with large misshapen turquoise stones intermingled with baubles, glass beads in pink, gold and green. Florine flipped it back into the box before walking away and I heard it rattle to the bottom, the sound similar to those made by intricate see-through gumball machines, where you can watch the coloured ball meander and clatter through a clear plastic path.

I watched Ingrid-Simone out of the corner of my eye as she disentangled. She began slowly, methodically, her hands in the box, fingers moving, her head off to the side, not even looking as she delved. She stood behind the front desk on the little stool we used to reach items hung on hooks close to the ceiling. A spotlight above and behind where I stood hanging up flowery frocks and cocktail dresses emanated a soft glow, a nimbus that appeared and disappeared as she moved to an unknown rhythm, a quotation that she was repeating in her head perhaps. I could see that she was deep in thought, somewhere else entirely, and I laughed softly when I saw her extract the long beaded necklace, or part of it, an umbilical cord. She put the end of it in her mouth, between her lips at first, then her teeth, as she continued to tease out the rest of the thing with her hands, invisible in the deep, slightly buckled cardboard.

I was watching an improvisation. A luminescence. A divination. Glass beads dripping from her lips, sparkling, casting bright colours, as she delicately and minutely moved her head in the clamour of daydream. Where was she? Her hands rummaging in the box, she a doctor in an emergency room, calm, otherworldly, in command of the universe. She removed a red pump, examined it for scuffs I imagine, marks that she would later remove. Set it down on the expanse of the desk. Continued.

I was smiling, so endearing was the scene, so dear the person, spaced out and absorbed at once. I hoped for her that there would be some lovely purses in the box amid all the other jumble that would amuse and delight her and send her off on her usual unexpected tangents. I predicted, awaited, a pleasant afternoon, listening to Ingrid-Simone recite bits of poems, quotations, ready to accompany her on whatever flights of fancy were inspired by the contents of this container. Maybe then I realized I was living her life moment by moment, that I had become hooked, addicted even to this kind of unfolding, this curious truth that was I.s.

It was a blur, the purse that she birthed from the wilting cardboard box. I was fiddling around, trying to get a recalcitrant dress to hang properly, to drape, and it was giving me some trouble, so my attention to Ingrid-Simone was temporarily taken away from me. Why do I think things might have been different if I'd been watching?

There was a kind of red blur, I saw that she had taken a large red handbag out and clutched it to her breast. I smiled to myself, I thought, lovely, she's found something then, and continued for a minute before looking up again.

She was in a new state, altered. I looked up from the dress I was wrangling and saw her face, a look of sorrow so intense that it read as terror, as though she had encountered a malevolent ghost. This thought entered me, drove into me, pierced me—that her heart had been broken, not just broken but also wholly massacred.

I went to her, walked, walked as though I was pulling my feet out of mud. A very large part of me wanted to turn away, bury my head in the dress rack, pretend I saw nothing, felt nothing. I wanted badly to not have seen this, to not have to enter whatever I was about to enter. I wished it away, strongly. I already knew everything would be different in our slight lives, our wildly insignificant lives, even if not another living soul noticed. It seemed that all I could focus on was the front counter; I have the exact colour of it etched in my mind, the large scratch that ran down the middle of it where so many people had run their hands, a wound they helped erase, smooth away. I saw the tall cardboard box in my mind, close to it as I was then. I remember the corrugations, the bulging out at the bottom, and the wilted flowering at the top. A water stain darkened an area on the side in the shape of a heart; honestly it was a heart. All that winter, working with Ingrid-Simone, this shape would appear and appear, though I took little note of it at the time and only now looking back does it seems meaningful. Heart and soul, have they not always gone together?

She sank. Behind the box, behind the counter, and when I reached her she was in a squat position, confronting heaven knows what. Was I equal to this, to watch over her suffering? I wasn't. I actually confessed this to my entrails; deep inside I cried this. I am not equal, I won't be, I refuse. And, why am I here? This is not my realm. I cursed myself for having left the academy and for now being so incredibly unimportant, and in the same breath, for connecting myself to someone equally unimportant. I promised myself to learn to keep distant from people. From Ingrid-Simone.

Smiling, it was almost a smile, I walked toward her curled up body, shrimp-curved spine, head on knees, below hair, soundless. This magic silence—we were plunged into another dimension. I forgave myself quickly for the thoughts of easy abandonment I had wished for as I met this sea creature huddled behind the great reef of our front desk. Had I not just pledged to watch over her? But that was when she was giving to me—the warmth and joy of her spirited and wise innocence.

I examined these moments later that night from the comfort of my turquoise chair, passing them off, saying, yes, you are only a human and humans have the capacity for small monstrosities, quick betrayals, of creating distances like chasms. I let myself off the hook very easily because it was only a brief betrayal. Only a thought.

I had wanted to exist only in the moment that winter without worrying or feeling responsible for anyone or to anything. How's that for the slipperiness of the soul? I could hear the sea foam crashing at the door and seeping seeping, so that my next thought was: I must get her off the floor. She must stand, must not drown, she will breathe.

I put my arm around her, her arm over my shoulder and she clutched the red blur of a handbag to her bleeding breast, the two merged together into a river of sheer pain, screaming, the colours pierced my ears as we walked slowly, as though she were her old, forgetful mother. I walked her to one of the fitting rooms and heard the bell jingle, the front door opened and some liquid-lunching ladies frolicked and bubbled into the store. I called out, —hello, welcome to Theodora's, I'll be right with you, over my shoulder as we inched forward.

I curtsied as I set her down, a dead weight, and heard her chant, not Rumi as I expected, but a psalm. Faint at first. My soul—breaketh—for longing—of thee. This is when I first knew that she was truly breathing and in her breaths were airy words, wispy.

My soul breaketh for longing of Thee. My soul breaketh for longing of Thee. My soul breaketh for longing of Thee. My soul breaketh for longing of Thee.

I would later remember that this very phrase was one of the epigraphs to Clarice Lispector's book, *Soulstorm*.

I set her down, propped her against the wall, and drew the heavy, blood-red and gold brocade curtains three-quarters closed, so that she would have air and so that I could see her as I walked by. I promised to get her a glass of water. I turned my attention to the lunching ladies. In my mind's eye, I saw her as a blur, a vague crimson, though she was completely still, stone still. The store was suddenly full of browsers, of ladies who wanted to try things on. A couple of them made a fuss over having found the exact dress that one of their society cohorts had worn to a certain gala. There was a line-up for the fitting rooms. Not a soul mentioned the half-open room, the one containing the young woman curled up, looking at the handbag in her arms, whispering to herself.

—Where the hell is Florine, I muttered. I popped my head into the back room when I got a chance but she had disappeared.

After the lunching ladies had dispersed, around mid-afternoon, Florine reappeared. I told her what had happened, where Ingrid-Simone was sitting. She was incredibly sensitive to the situation, very quiet, saying, —we shall close the store, then help her up and walk her home. Usually a distant, gruff person, a stony person, Florine softened in that moment into the woman I had had that brief encounter with in the hayfield. She put on a big wool button-up sweater, the kind that someone has to make for you. The buttons were wooden and worn and the wool was a muddy grey that tricks you into thinking it is almost purple. I swear I smelled sun-warmed hay as she pulled Ingrid-Simone's coat around her, pulling her forward and putting her arms into the sleeves, as you would dress an infant.

Florine nodded for me to wait. I had dressed in my winter coat and crocheted toque and Florine returned in a minute with her coat on as well. Ingrid-Simone, still hugging the purse, leaned against me—the way a large dog will lean against its human, as a sign of their connection, trust, as an opportunity for the human to scratch behind ears, to let that happen.

We walked her home in the winter's early dark, Florine holding one arm, and me the other. We neither of us had any idea where she lived, only that it wasn't terribly far. We set off in the direction Ingrid-Simone always took when she went home. At each corner we asked which way, and she whispered, straight or left or right. Six or seven blocks later we arrived at a four-story walk-up crowded out by high-rises. I reached into her coat pocket for her keys since Florine was carrying both her own bag and

Ingrid-Simone's too. We got her to the fourth floor, a slow climb in circles so that it felt like we were inside of a turret. We got her into her apartment and sat her at the kitchen table. Florine made tea while I slipped Ingrid-Simone's coat off, setting it behind her on the vintage chair complete with crocheted cosies for the feet designed to save the linoleum from scratches.

Florine found soda crackers in the cupboard and a flowery china plate, and set them down beside the toaster on the table. She poured tea into a pastel pink mug. Then she tenderly prised the handbag from Ingrid-Simone's fingers. I can still hear the sound of my gasp, coming from deep within me, and this surprised me also, the force of it. My surprise made audible. I realized then that we would take the purse with us, the red purse that Ingrid-Simone had birthed from the cardboard box that afternoon.

Florine said, —we'll go, then. I stroked Ingrid-Simone's arm and she nodded and so we left. I followed Florine and it seemed to be the right thing to do. When I looked over my shoulder, I could see Ingrid-Simone's lips move too, my soul breaketh for longing of Thee.

On the street, I turned around to see if I could make out which window was hers. Her kitchen table was near the window and I could see a figure holding a teacup as though she were about to take a sip, not yet at her lips, hovering. I took a moment to look at the building, so I would remember which one it was, and was quite stunned by its architecture. From the 1960s I imagined, but quite subtly designed to echo a castle, with hints of turrets on either end, the bricks at the top of the building laid in an interlacing pattern, giving the illusion of crenellations. The name scrolled on the front of the building was *The Royal Parzival*.

❧

You might think that the next day would have been strained or confessional or intimately dramatic. That we would descend into a woeful silence. Or all be visibly altered. But instead, it was as usual. When we got into the store,

Ingrid-Simone took off her long coat to reveal a beautiful outfit. Pencil skirt and fitted jacket in Robin's egg blue. A black turtleneck and thick black hose and tall vinyl boots.

—Look, she said, —and there's even a matching hat, which she took out of her bag and pinned into her hair, a 1950s affair with netting that she artfully arrayed. —Oh, and there's matching gloves, let me show you, they're just priceless, a scream really, and she dug them out of her bag. —I bought them at the thrift store, the whole shebang came in a traveling box, I'm sure none of it has ever been worn, and the case is mint, wonderfully pristine. I know there's a story there, don't you think? Hmmmmm.

I had arrived at the store a bit early on purpose. Florine was already there. I wanted to see the handbag up close. I had an insatiable urge, a frantic desire, to look inside it and feel its reverberations, what I imagined to be its very own aftershock. The day before, Florine had spirited it away, and to me it seemed as if she had accomplished some magic trick to make it disappear. —It's in the bottom of the filing cabinet, she said and let me look at it while she hovered in the doorway to the office.

The filing cabinet was wooden, from days gone by. Greasy and smoky-dark, cavernous. Heavy too, the previous tenant must have decided to leave it rather than struggle with it up the narrow back staircase. Maybe they had wanted something more modern, cheap metal. I opened the drawer; it slid out so smoothly. The purse, I looked at it for a moment in the depths, in its cocoon. Florine had forced it in so that it was crumpled on the sides. It was large but not huge. Long and quite narrow. More narrow than a doctor's bag, though it reminded me of that. Slightly less structured. Red, faux crocodile. There was a buckle clasp and also a zipper. Inside, I saw it was lined with paisley. I felt it, and it was very soft but not like silk, more plush. Brushed cotton, I guessed. There was one zippered side compartment, very discrete; I almost overlooked it. Otherwise, it was roomy, empty, a hollow. I closed it and hefted it by its handles. Took a few steps. Imagined walking down the street with it. Shopping with it. I don't know why. I imagined walking with it in Paris, walking by the Louvre, the Opera. Or in Rome, approaching the Coliseum down some side road.

I closed my eyes, held it in my arms, cradled it. I don't know what I was doing. I put it back in the bottom drawer and it closed rapidly when I nudged it with my boot. Reminded me of the drawers at morgues, though I've only ever seen such things on TV.

୧୬

We went on. And Ingrid-Simone was herself, though occasionally I still saw her lips moving and I knew she was reciting to herself, my soul breaketh.

As a test, I suppose it was a test, a few days later, I asked her for her favourite Rumi.

—"What is the soul," she said with a campy grin, her arms out, as she walked around the store, dramatically hiding behind a rack of dresses. —"I cannot stop asking." And here she took one off the rack, a long gown with flowing sleeves. She danced with the dress, fervently, spinning and spinning, dizzyingly so. —"If I could taste one sip of an answer, I could break out of this prison for drunks." So you see, she said, —we are all of us prisoners, drunks, her wild choreography taking her to the front desk, which she jumped onto with ease. I couldn't help but think of the box, the purse, all of the births that occur in a life.

—We are, I said, —oh how we are. I thought without despair about my limitations, then. I thought about how my shortcomings, or maybe let's call them truths, were what brought me there, that the various faltering paths I had set out on had convened, so that my falterings were what brought me to that particular truth. The truth that was Ingrid-Simone, that is I.s. Capital I, small s.

I thought about the reasons I had decided not to continue as an academic, even as I mourned. I mourned, but it was a resolute mourning, a contented one, perversely contented. I had confronted who I was not, had come to know the contours and severe limits but also the reaches of my intelligence. In not becoming an academic, I came to understand my intellect, and knowing it, I had some strange feeling that I could make use of it in some unforetold yet important and sublimely insignificant way. I may have been deluded in this matter; I'm not sure.

A couple of weeks later I felt oddly compelled to visit the filing cabinet again. This filing cabinet, which had become a monument, a secret shrine. The thing that hid, this monolith in its dark corner with the dust bunnies that convene at its feet and are sent scuttling across the floor when the drawers open, heavy but with a whoosh, on their smooth, well-worn mechanism. Over the years this chest, this cabinet for files, has been patted, has heard: they don't make 'em like this anymore, no sirree. This greasy wooden beast, bovine, with its four stomachs, and the one that concealed, at the very bottom.

I had arrived fifteen minutes early, though this was unplanned, so I told myself. Ingrid-Simone usually arrived at the store a minute or two before it opened. When I arrived, Florine said she needed to go out and left. Her ghostly manner of taking leave was so quiet, so unobtrusive, that when she is gone you hardly believed she was there at all.

For some reason, I imagined the drawer wouldn't open, that it had been locked. When I pulled on it, I didn't expect it to give. But it did, it slid out cleanly. Minutes passed. I could see it there, huddled, foetal, wedged, and yet the handbag seemed more expansive than I remembered. The purse a belly that has let out its breath, has at last stopped trying to suck in its gut. Relaxed. It had moulded itself into the space allotted. And yet I sensed internal tremblings, contractions, a lustre, the silent rumbling an egg will make before hatching. As I withdrew the purse from the compartment, I was overwhelmed by vertigo, laden with possibility.

This is what I think must have happened. As I bent down, grasped the purse by its handles, pulled gently gently, it filled sideways with air. I yanked on it, with some force, and then increasing force, until it was expelled from that sliding passage, and I took a quick dance step backward, straightening up in the process. I was willing to accept magic. A spell was cast, then. I knew to open it, to feel along the inner seams. It contained. Suddenly, as they say, I understood. Less about what it contained, but that it did. I understood this purely metaphorically. But then my fingers, caressing, probing, compressing and then sliding over the innards of this hidden purse, discerned.

⁊

My fingers discerned.

The purse a belly that had let out its breath. Expelled. Along the bottom of the purse there was a pocket, unzipped. Impossible to see because of the darkness, because of the busy-ness of the paisley pattern. I only knew because of my tentative foray into the depths. What compelled me to remain there, an unevenness, a slight imbalance? I reached into what was a fold, sewn into the pocket, an interval of fabric that was designed to hold whatever contents, preventing them from sliding out, from being born.

I reached in. I birthed a thin sheaf of papers, without thinking about the repercussions, without asking myself, are you sure? I reached into the extreme silence of the handbag, into the paisley abyss, into the wound of this side compartment, and withdrew. I replaced the purse, the placenta, for now it appeared to me as a mode or passage, a path, an arcane and sultry innocence. I looked down and noticed what I held, then. A leather folder, kid goat, softest leather, so very thin. A fold within the fold from the depths. And then I entered a silence so vast.

⁊

I took the leather folder and placed it into my own purse. Ingrid-Simone arrived just as I was hiding it. I hid it from her. Smiling, nonchalant, I turned toward her, welcoming, with my hand in my purse, fumbling. I put my purse in the cupboard behind the front desk, which is where I always put my purse.

—I have something for you today, said Ingrid-Simone. Then she slipped elegantly out of her long black Mary Poppins coat and draped it over the counter. She handed me a plain shopping bag with handles, very light. Red and tangerine tissue artfully brimming out of the bag, like licks of fire.

—You didn't! I said. She nodded happily, vigorously.

—Open, open, open! She responded. And I did. Another miniature purse, I knew this, reaching into the fiery paper. A bit larger than the Woolf purse. This one was black. An old-fashioned tag with thick twine hung from it on which she had written, "...to her left a capacious black bag, shopping variety, and to her right a collapsed parasol..." On the bag itself, she had embroidered the name Winnie, and once again her own initials were embroidered below, hardly visible. So this was the bag from Beckett's *Happy Days*. Do not overdo the bag, Winnie.

On the back of the tag there were words, a list. She pointed this out to me, wordlessly, her lips pursed, inward. She seemed to be calm and jittery both at once.

> toothbrush, toothpaste
> small mirror
> spectacles
> bottle of red medicine
> lipstick
> magnifying glass
> comb/brush
> revolver
> unidentifiable odds and ends
> musical box
> nail file

When I fumbled open the petite bag, which nevertheless seemed huge, weighty, I found the contents of the list. I examined each thing, each exquisite object, the red medicine bottle, the music box. I wondered and laughed over the unidentifiable odds and ends. And then we remembered that we had to open the store and ran to the front door to let in an elderly lady, walking with a cane, stomping her boots on the front carpet as she came in. —In my day, she lectured us, —we were always punctual. That meant something. And we were silent, and looked at each other without any expression at all and said nothing to her. Nothing for a good long time. I put the Beckett purse back in the bag, wrapping it carefully in the tissue and nestled it by my own purse in the cupboard.

☙

What day did I write: I haven't considered her a friend. There was no giddiness about the way we connected, no need to analyse or label. Maybe there was relief from the usual obligations of friendship, of named relationships, because we were co-workers. Co-workers manage a distance between each other that is generally understood to be a wise rule. You don't go out for coffee, or have each other over for tea, setting out the China that was left to you by your grandmother and rushing out to buy biscuits that might tantalize.

I had not considered her a friend but it did not mean she wasn't a friend. Were we kindred spirits of some sort then? Some as yet undefined permutation of friends? Soul-sisters? Certainly a permutation. I copied out a quotation from Nietzsche on a scrap of paper, "It is not how one soul approaches another but in how it distances itself from it that I recognize their affinity and relatedness." We were two souls who were diligent at keeping a certain distance from each other. At first I worried that it was just me who needed distance, but Ingrid-Simone was also artful. I knew that though she still fawned over the handbags and purses that came in, we were not really to talk about them. I noticed that when she was selling them, she seemed desperate to see them go, to clear them out of her sight but also call them back if she could. There was a longing that she banished from her gaze, sometimes with a literal blink of the eyes.

When I tried to approach the subject of the miniature purses she made, she became a bit secretive, danced away from the subject, making some joke or gliding over to a customer that she might have easily ignored for another little bit. She once told me that each one took weeks, and she dressed up in attire that might match the purse at hand. Tweeds and serviceable shoes, or wide brimmed hats and vintage heels from the 1950s.

We were uniquely bonded in the way that intelligent-enough people are when they work in jobs that others might consider being 'beneath them.' Theodora's was a refuge for us, a place to breathe, to regroup and maybe to hide for a while. We laughed though, at the way some people talked to us. At times slowly and loudly, enunciating for us lowly shopgirls their demands. I often received more of the condescending and patronizing remarks than Ingrid-Simone did, because customers must have assumed that someone my age working in a second-hand store must not be able to find anything else while a younger person could be there working while she went to college. Or at least she had the hope of making something of herself.

Ingrid-Simone was constantly amazed at my restraint, —you're so Zen, she would drawl when a woman wearing plastic-surgery induced sunglasses handed me her paper coffee cup and said, —dispose of this. No please, no thank you, no could you possibly… just, dispose of this. Partially shocked at this type of behaviour, I found it interesting to observe in my camou-flaged, anonymous state. Or so I told myself. Ingrid-Simone rolled her eyes and said, —Oh, I almost blew your cover and told her myself that you're researching a book, and that you have twelve university degrees no less, and that you're the most brilliant person I know. And then she laughed a musical and outraged laugh that made the experience of being handed a trickle of brown liquid in a lipstick-smudged paper cup unfathomably mysterious and almost philosophically profound. As though together we had confronted the awkward and lopsided order of the world and arrived at a grandiose compassion for all those who existed on one side or the other, all because of the woman with dark owl glasses, thick legs, and tight skin. Because we each knew how to exist as someone we weren't and to fool them in this way. And better, we could keep the secret quite well.

❧

But my calling is also to dream. While writing this, reconstructing and concocting, I take naps to dream my way toward remembering things I forgot to write down. I don't really sleep; my naps are more of a lucid daydream. This is difficult work, so sometimes I arise more tired than when I lay down. During a nap, one time, I remembered Ingrid-Simone telling me that she also likes to nap but not very often because dreaming in the afternoon frightened her. She said to me, —I take a little Diet Coke before having an afternoon nap. That way my dreams are more awake, more effervescent, and once in a while I put pop rocks in my mouth just as I'm lying down. Then my dreams sparkle as well.

Occasionally I walked around the store and heard crackling and never remembered what it was until I came upon Ingrid-Simone. I walked around thinking there must be a mouse or an electrical short. And then there would be Ingrid-Simone, steaming a ruffled pirate shirt, her mouth full of pop rocks. She would put her hand in front of her mouth and try not to laugh and shrug her shoulders. When they finished crackling, she would say, — oh, I couldn't help it. I'm such a child, aren't I?

❧

Have I mentioned the Sylvia Plath purse? Ingrid-Simone had read the poem, "Wuthering Heights." The ending goes like this,

The grass is beating its head distractedly.
It is too delicate
For a life in such company;
Darkness terrifies it.
Now, in valleys narrow
And black as purses, the house lights
Gleam like small change and pace.
Inside the small black purse was a scene, the sheep, the heather, the
narrow valleys, the house lights that gleam like small change.

❧

I don't want to leave things out. Recording all the moments that made up our winter at Theodora's could be someone's life work, a thousand pages. I want you to remember that there was not a single tragic thing about her those months of cold and snow and freezing rain. After a warm day, the rain began to fall half an hour maybe before closing time. We watched it on the front window, sliding slowly and stickily down. Changing the shapes of the drifts we could see, melting things, blurring the edges, turning the white snow into a grainy, grimy substance that had more in common with a Sno-Cone than our former winter wonderland. When we walked out the front door, the temperature had dropped; it was quite dark and the sidewalk was slippery, exceedingly so.

—Oooooh! How dangerous! said Ingrid-Simone with a gleam in her eye. —Let's find a slope.

—No really, I tried to explain to her, —this is dangerous, just as you said.

—The trick, she replied, —is to embrace it, to slide. And so we slid to a point a couple of blocks away where there was a defined slope and the sidewalk was glistening—in a state between being completely frozen and shiny-wet under the streetlights. She crouched down and instructed me to do the same, behind her, then to grip onto her waist, so that we formed a train. One gentleman walked by us on the edge of the sidewalk where there was snow to walk in for traction, looking down, and fired off an, —okay? as he hurried by.

—Yes, yes, said Ingrid-Simone, though I'm not sure he heard or cared to. We went down a couple of times, sprawling out at the bottom of the slope, which was longer than it appeared from the top, and stumbled up laughing through the crunchy wet snow. We stood apart, she on the snow on one side of our icy track that was the sidewalk and I on the other.

Snow started to fall then. Icy, sharp flakes. We complained about them and remarked on how our cheeks were smarting and talked about the changeability of the weather like two little old ladies, which made us laugh at ourselves. We were illuminated somewhat by a nearby streetlight and the sound of traffic on the street over was a dull hum. Even so I thought I heard Ingrid-Simone gasp, for as I was making gestures with my sage green be-mittened hand about the ridiculousness of rain followed by such mean little flakes of snow, a black feather fell from the sky and I saw that she was pointing at my hand, which for some reason unknown to me even now, I was holding out.

A black feather fell from the early dark sky and came to me, I, who was waiting for it, unbeknownst. Unbeknownst, I received.

Strange, but when I remember the feather coming to me now, I can really see it, in my mind's eye, as it fell, falling through the twinkling snow, a breath illuminated. Even though in reality I never looked up and it appeared magically, without warning or premonition, I can see it so clearly, spiralling, dizzy, can feel the warbling vibrations, the soft breath of the universe in its serene passage from sky to mitten.

Ingrid-Simone was sure it was a good omen, but all I could say was, —but, it's black.

She said, —you know very well that black does not equal evil and white does not equal good.

—Yes, you have me on that kid, I replied.

I carried the feather cupped between my two mittens as we walked on the boulevards in the now-biting snow. We parted eventually and I took my black feather home and placed it on the windowsill and asked it questions. And I listened to it breathe, my black feather with its breath like Pegasus.

Ingrid-Simone came bounding into work the next day with what she said was the message.

—The message, she said, —the message is: the guardian of your soul is near. And she repeated slowly, as though I were a child, —the guardian of your soul is near. Your SOUL.

She had Googled 'black feather' and 'meaning' and this was the top result, and as it was a perfect one too, she had ended her search right there. —This means you're the guardian of my soul, then, doesn't it? I said to her. —But what if you were meant to receive it, and I just happened to stick my hand out and ruin it all?

I was in a silly mood that morning after my long evening of brooding and talking to a feather, even if it had been an internal dialogue. I wanted to shake myself out of any seriousness that might lead to being gloomy. But Ingrid-Simone was intense in her need to discuss the feather and our responsibilities as guardians. If she were to be the guardian of my soul, she would not take the assignment lightly, but she couldn't help but feel that the message indicated a more mystical force at work, a mystical guardian who would take care of my soul. And might extend that sort of guardianship around whoever was near.

For myself, I had already understood the message. I understood that the message of the black feather was that Ingrid-Simone was the guardian of my soul. I had already known this and the feather was a confirmation of that. And it reminded me of how we come to know things and reminds me now.

I'm trying to make sense of how certain moments in our encounters with each other were so exactly like a Polaroid snapshot, a Polaroid portrait.

Muted, and slightly more yellow than other moments, and I have to squint at them and shake them slightly to see if they're finished developing because they seem to need more time. And though I cannot put it into words at all, no not at all, at the time, I knew I was experiencing something that changed my chemical make-up in some small but significant manner. Afterwards, there was a constant bittersweetness in the company of those who inhabited the frame, a sidelong feeling, like a half-smile—full of an extraordinary and yet tolerated sadness, but at precisely the same time, a pure kind of content-ment. I am full of a blind kind of knowing, a gratefulness even.

The Polaroid shot I have of Ingrid-Simone in my mind is of her stand-ing in front of me, snow on her eyelashes, as we stared at the black feather on my mitten. Of the snow coming down and the streetlight illuminating an area over her left shoulder. And it feels like I knew then that I would be sitting where I am now, looking back at this moment and holding it in my mind's eye as a treasure, a wistful moment that doesn't dare to be longing. When I say longing, it's a longing for myself, who I was then or whom I hoped I would be. It's a longing to be whom I was when I was with her and knowing it will not be repeated. All of her kindnesses that winter, the kindness one confers merely by being, the magic sometimes in that.

೨

The day following the arrival of the black feather, there was a snowstorm. We spent some time worrying about Florine and talking about the way our worrying about her and our observations of winter coincided. What did we know about winter, about predicting the weather? We were absurdly, randomly, attempting to fill the gaps of the unknown, all those things we would never know about Florine, with snow.

The window was bright with falling snow that day and we were alone and worried about Florine walking through the storm, lost. Even though she very often left us for a day and never phoned, we still wondered. Ingrid-Simone said we liked to know where she was at all times because of the strange relationships we each had with our mothers, mine the agoraphobe and hers with early-onset Alzheimer's, locked on the third floor of a seniors home where they keep all the people with dementia who don't know themselves or their loved ones anymore. As for Florine, we were not sure if she liked the element of surprise, so it seemed to us, or if she was merely absent-minded and didn't think we were troubled by her comings and goings.

No one had come by Theodora's that morning except the postal carrier and we decided to make tea and refuse to do any work, not that there was much to do. Ingrid-Simone sat on the front counter and I brought out the crimson velvet armchair from the dressing rooms. A large shape entered the store in a whorl of wind and snow and cold. We had to shake our heads to see what it was when the door finally closed with an exaggerated suckling sound. A man, bundled in so many layers, hat, scarf, immense black puffy coat, came in carrying an object wrapped in a garbage bag. Not clothes—that we could see immediately.

He had brought in an old typewriter, a Remington, that someone had painted red, likely destroying its value for collectors. He wordlessly placed it on the table beside the front counter where we usually displayed shoes and hats and jewellery, though we hadn't gotten around to doing so yet. Wordlessly, he unwrapped it and we watched. Then the three of us stood staring at it without exchanging any words. Ingrid-Simone looked at me with such mischief in her eyes, just as I was about to say the standard line, I'm sorry but we're only looking for high quality, cleaned and pressed clothing, as well as accessories, also in excellent condition.

—Lovely, said Ingrid-Simone, and then, —hmmmmm, so softly.

And the man said, —yours if you want it, don't want anything for it, no room at home. Okay?

Very little was said after this and he soon left, and there we were, left with a typewriter, brilliantly red, an utterly mad red. Ingrid-Simone went to work right away, finding paper, threading it around the spool. The ribbon was still inky enough and she began to type.

—The severe tranquillity of snow.

—Fragrance swathed.

She told me that for her, snow had a scent, a fragrance, an odour, an ardour. And that each kind of snow was particular in its scent.

She typed:

Fresh mint, basil and lime, ash and grass.

Apples, roses, marigold, Roger's Golden Syrup.

Soft poached eggs, yeast, dank and mossy wolf.

When it melts—salt and butter.

An old-fashioned chocolate malt, creamy and grainy.

Lemongrass.

Sunnyboy cereal with cream and brown sugar.

Vinegar in a bucket for washing the floors.

And then she proceeded to talk about the kinds of snowflakes, and typed these also. —There is calm snow, oh, how I love calm snow! There is the snow of departures with its innumerable question marks. She spoke and typed in intervals. —Hmmmmm. Then, there is the snow that is breath, oh, yes, you know it by listening to the calligraphy of how it carves itself into previous snowfalls. And let's not forget, cosmic snow, delicate and elegant, tinged with an otherworldly pink and blue. And the sugary plumage, the powder, of anguished snow.

—The large, softly floating flakes with their otherworldly exuberance, these are consolations. They float easily to those who need them most. The pale and sunshiny crystals, those belong to certain old people, who understand the bite and brilliance together because they have lived so fully and for so long.

—Sleet belongs to those who will be arriving home to hot cocoa. The snow that falls when the sun is going down is a comfortable snow, soothing. The intermittent and gentle snow that exists solely to put roses in the cheeks of small children, that is a benediction, a fluttering of angels.

We left her notes in the typewriter and maybe Florine read them the next time she came in, wondering why there was a typewriter on the table by the front desk. But we knew by then that she wouldn't say anything. We made it part of the display and soon it became a fixture at the store. Ingrid-Simone said maybe she'd take it home in the spring and that sounded fine.

♥

I learned to be patient with Ingrid-Simone. I learned patience from her. Not that she required patience, quite the opposite. I could see that when I waited, if I was quiet and listened more, Ingrid-Simone shone, which is not a word I use lightly. She was radiant at times. The thing is, I actually felt—patient. An inner calm. And I had never felt that before and I know it was because of Ingrid-Simone.

That was the winter we asked questions about the soul and held them in our mouths like toffee, the winter we made a home in the obliquely hopeful consigned discards of the second-hand clothing store. A colourful nest, soft and worn and always changing.

How to set the direction of the soul? The soul's compass? We began with the words of Simone Weil, "If the soul is set in the direction of love... the nearer we approach to the beauty of the world." Was this our goal? To approach nearer to the beauty of the world? Were our souls properly set in the direction of love? How can one come near to the reality of another's soul? And in my mind, I also asked, what is the reality of Ingrid-Simone's soul? I'm still asking, will always be asking.

We loved Emily Dickinson's lines, "Hope is the thing with feathers / That perches in the soul." I know I believed in hope, the feathery thing.

But did Ingrid-Simone? She talked about the desire to hope, wanting, wishing for this belief. She believed in the guardian of her soul and she believed in the beauty of the world, that much was clear.

☙

She would turn into a bird, by knitting a blue-grey, sky-bright sweater with a pattern of overlapping feathers and throwing it over herself as she ran down a hill. There you would see her transform into an imposing bird with an impressive wingspan.

Maybe I wrote those lines on the day she received a ticket for jaywalking. The same day she gave me a letter in a small envelope, addressed in a handsome swirling calligraphy, flourishes and all. Inside was a folded sheet no larger than a postage stamp. Unfolded, the word: Live. Which I knew must be from Rumi and of course it was. This was exactly what I needed to hear and I slipped it into my pocket straight away and carried it with me every day. Here it is right now with me.

But what Ingrid-Simone received that day was a traffic ticket for jaywalking and it destroyed her. You're either the sort of person who is going to understand why or you're not, so the only thing I can do is help you imagine what she looked like crossing the street and let you see why this should not have been a violation, at least not in this instance.

She was a young anonymous woman running elegantly reckless across a street with a slight slope. The snow was swirling all around her heels and she held her coat tight around her neck with her left hand. Of course her scarf was flying behind her. The indecent plumes of exhaust from the cold cars were beautiful, you couldn't help but interpret them that way. You see, she was just about to take flight; she was about to fly into the low grey clouds, when a whistle blew and a woman appeared out of nowhere, a woman in uniform. Made a hundred times worse because it was a female cop, she had to relinquish her perfect anonymity to someone with no regard for such things but who ought to have understood that her hiding place had been stirred up and mangled, her perfect hiding spot in the middle of a busy city street taken away. She had forgotten her gloves that day and the wind was biting into her as she stood still, receiving the ticket, her hands red and chapped, everyone walking by with dead eyes and not a single look of sympathy, not even one. Did they not imagine that she'd been carrying a message that said: Live.

She was swindled that morning by the statuary of a female cop and by everyone who walked by, swindled out of life and living and dreaming for an entire morning. Did they not see that she had been ready to take flight? That there was a sublime disturbance in the air having to do with the sprouting of fine grey and pure white feathers, the fibre and tendrils of her being about to soar into a remote and nourishing invisibility. Into a dynamic and intoxicating swoon of pre-flight delirium. The particles of the air that held her were already whispering to each other. I can still feel the vibrations hatching.

There. That's enough. Oh my darlings this is enough. Just tell me you will, you will heed the message of the dense and gentle sky: live. Live.

✧

I myself don't want the disruption of those whose soul lacks luminosity.

Do you know how much confidence it takes some days to write a single sentence on a pale yellow post-it note? If I have had such days, such moments of confidence, it's only because of Ingrid-Simone.

✧

Another thing about her, her hair. I remember it as often being greasy and occasionally quite oily. This oddly only made her more attractive. The sort of neglect that suggested that her life outside the store was full and wild and exotic. In truth I knew very little about her life outside the store. I knew she often went to the library to seek refuge and obscure knowledge. She called it knowledge roulette. A game of chance that she herself made up and could change the rules to suit the situation, the combination of books she found. To see what would find her if she put herself on one path or another. To see what might stick.

We were certainly odd though, different from everyone who came into the store. Most of these women painted their nails, had expensive haircuts, and wore lipstick from the cosmetic counter and not the drugstore. Some of them were fashionable young things, dressed half in expensive designer clothes and half in what they called 'vintage' clothes. Their shoes were always impeccable.

The women dropping off their clothes wore more perfume than those who shopped for them we noticed, though sometimes these were the same women. Neither Ingrid-Simone nor I painted our nails. We cut our own hair when we cut it at all. Once when the store wasn't very busy, Ingrid-Simone walked up to me with scissors and said, —cut me some bangs, you know, a fringe, just straight across. So we put scotch tape on her hair and I cut. She was stunning. Not that I can take the credit. She was so pleased with her free haircut.

Ingrid-Simone often wore red lipstick. She wore it perfectly, as though it belonged on her. There was never feathering, or smudging, or lipstick on her teeth. I often wanted to ask her what colour and brand she wore, but I always forgot. As for me, I always wore neutral make-up. Lightest shades of lipstick and pale eye shadow.

—When I was a child, Ingrid-Simone told me, —I called eye shadow, cry shadow.

I wore foundation but it too was pale. The lines under my eyes were really starting to be visible but I found them interesting and wanted to see how they were going to develop over the years. I remembered reading somewhere that Georgia O'Keeffe once had a makeover by Elizabeth Arden, who was a patron of O'Keeffe's art. O'Keeffe couldn't get home fast enough to wash it off. I told this story to Ingrid-Simone, who had never heard of O'Keeffe, so that night she looked her up on the internet. The next morning, she pronounced her the most beautiful woman she had ever seen, so wholly real. Knowing and serene.

—Oh, Shaya, I'm still swooning, like a honeybee that dipped and bumbled into so many flowers last night! What a world of delight and mystery. How wise O'Keeffe must have been, for only someone who was a true seer could have painted such flowers. I felt as though they were portals, hmmmmm, I looked at one red flower for ages, and you know, I could have walked into it, maybe I fell into it. Like Alice in Wonderland. I was at home, you know?

Her newfound interest in O'Keeffe, which I was proud to have stirred up in her, resulted in a miniature purse shaped like the skull of a cow. And inside there was a washcloth and an empty change purse, since she had read that O'Keeffe never kept money in her purse. But an enormous and vibrant red flower took up most of the purse. It was designed so that when you took it out, it was a small red dot, but this unfolded, blossomed, right before your very eyes, opening, opening...

❧

She nearly made herself ill some days talking about her growing need, her compulsion to get to the Museum of Bags and Purses. The only thing that unwound her was the self-analysis of her compulsion. Trying to understand compulsions in general, why so many people have such strong desires to go somewhere they've never been. And how you always hear people say things like, "I felt at last that I was home," when you read travelogues.

—There's an exhibit you see, and it's only there until the end of January and I dearly want to see it, but it's the beginning of January and well, you know it won't happen, but it torments me all the same. It's called

For your eyes only: the secrets of the bag, and it's all about the private contents of women's bags. That's what it says on the website. I don't have to tell you, Shaya, how I was both so thrilled to read about it and at the same time utterly bloody vanquished by it.

—Oh, I'm embarrassed to tell you how long I spent on Google street view last night, she said. —How futile it is, how incredibly exquisitely frustrating. It's not enough, constantly seeing that front door, and never being able to open it. I want to know how it smells when you first enter the foyer, what the door handle feels like in my hand.

She wondered about what to wear and decided on something classic but elegantly nondescript. She imagined walking up to the museum, feeling dizzy, dreamy, as though she were sleepwalking. She worried that looking at it so often on street view would not make it seem real when she finally did make it there.

—I have this recurring dream. I'm in the museum and it's the middle of the night. I open all the purses, the Judith Lieber cupcake purse, the crystal-encrusted Diet Coke purse by Kathrine Baumann, the Normandie, the peacock-feathered bag, the shiny red bag by Alexander McQueen, and I can hear them sigh one large collective sigh. And then, I'm taken in by an inward breath. In my dream, suddenly I'm drawn into this huge breath, transcendent; there is a vast and silent warble, so acute and patient, that I interpret as God.

❦

I began to think about her in my dreams. At some point during the winter, she crept into me, as though for warmth. Her voice. Her hmmmms. Her hymns. I would hear her breathe in dreams without images. It was a comfort. I became more silent as winter went on. I attempted to explain it. I had read there was a culture in which the women became silent after the age of forty. I felt I was approaching a very deep silence and I didn't know how long it would last but I wanted it, felt myself moving into it, that inner quiet, even though I couldn't quite understand it. But Ingrid-Simone accommodated it.

My silence was accommodated.

As I became quieter, we both became nervous also. There was an escalation in nerves, it seems to me now. She for her reasons, me for others. It made us compatible, each of us in our estrangement. We were vibrating on the same frequency, agitation on the brink.

There was an understanding, too, that we wouldn't infringe upon the other in the hours outside of our humble little jobs at Theodora's. We were delicate with each other in that way. There was a balance that we had achieved rather mysteriously, that we were not willing to throw off. We both felt that. I know we did.

∾

Listening to her talk about purses as she cleaned and polished them with such reverence was consoling. When I watched her, I became mournful. I was reminded of the way women used to wash corpses for burial, especially the feet. Loved ones or someone they knew, a part of their community. Not the way it is now, bodies shipped off into the mysteries of the funeral home to be looked after by strangers.

There was an intimacy, a respect, a profound sadness about her as she went about her task.

∾

Has it taken me this long to get back to the leather folder, hidden in the red handbag, the handbag that lead to Ingrid-Simone's crumbling? I have been reluctant to return to it. I had the folder of letters and bits of paper but I couldn't look at them. I held them; I had this feeling that I was holding them for her, holding the leather wallet. I carried it around with me everywhere, in my own purse now. Waiting. For when I felt that Ingrid-Simone would want to look at them, be strong enough for them, they seemed to belong to her, though who knows to whom they belonged. I had opened it, just a small increment, not even a centimetre. I saw handwriting. I closed it. I had this idea, this feeling, that one day she would ask to see the fawn-coloured folder, even though there was no way she could know about its existence.

❧

It takes me a while to put things together, but I realized that Ingrid-Simone's obsession with the private contents of handbags was not that dissimilar to my previous obsession with the secrets of women writers. Along with secrets though, I also wanted to know about sponge-cakes. Jane Austen wrote in a letter to her beloved sister Cassandra, "Which of all my important nothings shall I tell you first?" and later, "You know how interesting the purchase of a sponge-cake is to me."

The miniature Jane Austen purse that Ingrid-Simone made me was an intricately embroidered reticule in a silvery blue silk fabric, filled with a multitude of small, very small sponge-cakes.

❧

I want to write down every single quirky and delightful and awkwardly elegant thing I can think of about Ingrid-Simone. Before I get to the rest. I want to write down all of our conversations that took place in the brightness of new snow, her pure heart.

There was the morning that a very young woman wearing lofty boots teetered into the store with her baby. She looked at clothes for a while as she rocked and swayed with her baby in her arms. This seemed fine. Neither of us, I imagine, was the sorts to fuss over babies and coo and ask silly questions, or offer the advice that strangers give mothers. We just went about what we were doing. The baby started to cry rather shrilly and the mother looked anxious, flagging me over.

—It's so cold out, I don't want to sit in the car to breastfeed, is there anywhere I can sit? I'll be quick, she said

—Of course, I said, —you can use one of the change rooms, it's not busy. I pulled the velvet curtain and she asked if I could leave it partway open so it wouldn't get too stuffy.

—I can't stand stuffy, she said.

—Okay, no problem, I smiled, and left her, thinking little of the whole thing.

A small winter bird flew into our store that day. Maybe it had hopped in when someone had opened the door for another slower person. Feeling the warmth and measuring it against the drabness of its existence, the bird had taken a chance and entered in the blinding whoosh of a door opening in winter, leading into warmth however impossible.

The bird, my god, found the change room and flew inside. The bird conceded to fly in. Proceeded. This startled the young lady and there was commotion, the air was altered, stirred. Soft grey feathers were alight. The woman attempted to shoo the thing without disturbing her feeding babe. Her handbag fell, plunged, from the chair and spilled onto the floor and the child lost its grip on a moment of nourishing comfort as the mother bent over with the bundle in her arms and scooped her belongings. At this point, Ingrid-Simone walked by, shrieked, and ran out of the store with a look of abject terror on her face, though she returned quite composed fifteen minutes later.

Throughout the day though I noticed that she was humming more than usual, that her lips were moving subtly from time to time. And I knew it was 'my soul breaketh for longing of Thee.' She seemed spaced out, but fine, too. That was the day I came home and wrote on a note: sorrowbird.

The next day she came in with a rumpled paper grocery bag of her vintage romance novels and spent most of the day consuming packet after packet of pop rocks and reading, one romance after another. I think she read five that day. She made little attempt to work, and I said to her, —don't worry, I don't mind. And really I didn't.

Once in a while, I walked by her chair beside the front desk and without my asking she'd say, —this one is about Chase and Mackenzie and it's a classic case of amnesia. She's forgotten that he's really her mean-hearted boss, but after their car went off the road and they had to break into a cabin to stay alive, she's falling drastically and secretly in love with him. Of course, he's really not mean-hearted, but has been in love with her for a long time. But since she had a boyfriend, well. She was off limits. The trouble is he thinks she still has the boyfriend, and because she has amnesia, she can't tell him that they've broken off ages before. Naturally he's a terribly honourable sort of fellow and won't trespass on another guy's girl. It's made him seem nasty, but at heart he's quite a daaarling.

There was a glimmer of playfulness in her otherwise dry description, her dampened demeanour.

Then she showed me the cover, as I always enjoyed the covers, and went back to reading. I proceeded to put things on hangers that had been left in the fitting rooms the day before. Occasionally a customer would come in, and I sold a Chanel jacket to one older lady. A woman with fuchsia smudged lipstick came in looking for a handbag, throwing out names like Jean Paul Gautier, Coach, Prada, Hermès, Alexander McQueen, as though we were situated in New York City and not this buried-in-snow city in the absolute middle of nowhere. I thought the word, handbag, would enliven Ingrid-Simone, but she resolutely sank into her book, raising it so it covered her face, with no concern for anyone seeing her hide behind a picture of a woman in a nurse's uniform from the 1970s with a man looming in the background, his face chiselled, his hair perfect. Only if you looked very closely did you see he was holding a doctor's bag. So, I took this lady with the short, pink, down-filled jacket and heavily mascaraed eyes around and showed her the various purses we had. And she showed me the dress she had brought with her in her own monstrously huge satchel so we could match the colours.

ℰ℘

Through the winter, Ingrid-Simone ran out of her vintage romances and shifted to reading contemporary ones. Maybe we were two-thirds of the way through the winter, the cold. The early darkness had just started to retreat so there was more light, and some days seemed so intensely bright, the sun reflecting off the snow and leaving us squinting. This kind of light entered one in a way that it didn't at any other time of the year. This cold light, its brightness stark and lonely and severe entered us, sharp and clean and reminded us to agree with C.S. Lewis, that we do not have souls, we are souls.

—The contemporary romances, said Ingrid-Simone, —are so much more extravagant, embellished. I don't read them for plot; I'm not interested in plot in the least. I read them strictly for, here she paused and I jokingly said, —sex, whereupon she looked at me severely, then smiled with such lovely impish joy.

—For the loneliness and the emptiness and the longing that wants filling. I just read one where the protagonist had been a foster child, going from family to family, never feeling loved. Her entire life had been about wishing and longing and not daring to believe that she could be loved. What I most appreciated about this romance was the descriptions of clothes, of course she had lived in second-hand clothes all her life and her suitcases were so well-worn. Clichéd stuff I know but it focused my own longing, as through a cold crystal, and when she finally realizes she's loved in return, it was such a holy release for me, that I wept like a fool and felt so happy for a moment or two. Two beautiful minutes that felt real enough. If dreams are real in a way, if we can think of dreams as real, because we really had them and lived them, cannot this sort of happiness be as well?

—Oh, I'm so ashamed, Shaya! Romances are just so terrible, aren't they? Ingrid-Simone said with the widest eyes and her red lips in such a playful smile.

I could see that she wasn't ashamed, not really, and when I think of the way that she said the word ashamed, I could tell it was one she was intimate with. She was able to play with the word but I had the sense that she had said it in so many ways that she knew many of its sides, shapes and depths.

We went on from the discussion of romances to how winter longing is so beautiful and sweet and how that at times it made us inexplicably happy and gently sad, as well. Maybe because the return of green leaves reaching toward the sun was inevitable. The way the trees raised their arms in praise, a green scripture, slow and shimmery and patient, no matter what.

❧

Skip the rest, if you want. In fact, I won't mind if you stop right here. You already know everything important, everything I want you to know about Ingrid-Simone. I can't help but feel wretched and responsible for you now, if you go on with the story. That is, unless you are the sort of person who is consoled, once in a while, by imbibing in the unfortunate fragments of a young girl's story. If you are, I suppose we should talk about happiness again, right now.

All winter, we were happy, but not at the expense of losing our sadness. Not at the expense of forgetting that we were responsible for guarding each other's sorrows. We were each the guardians of one another's soul.

But what is the soul? The question persisted. I told Ingrid-Simone about the Steppenwolf treatise.

—The Steppenwolf at first believed he had two souls, one being of course the wolf soul, but no, I said, —in the treatise he learns that every human might consist "of ten, or a hundred, or a thousand souls." The many-flowered soul of the wolf. The treatise was considered to be a 'fortune telling booklet.'

And I wondered how many times Clarice Lispector had read the book. And if she re-read it before writing *The Hour of the Star*. Before writing the scene of Macabea and the fortune teller. Macabea and Madame Carlota. Ingrid-Simone and I talked about these books in the most random and un-academic way. I mentioned the cream-filled chocolates that Madame Carlota drops into her mouth and I mentioned her greasy face. I remembered somehow there were tramped-upon blades of grass, fiercely growing in the cracks of the pavement that Macabea notices before she enters the fortune teller's house. I told her how reading about the blades of grass growing in the cracks affected me. I had to put the book down. I had to pick it up again. A common image that is used to maximum effect. How does a writer do that, I wondered? Take a plain and weary image and make it mean so much.

—Maybe any time one reads about blades of grass growing in the cracks of pavement in the middle of winter, this will incomprehensibly disrupt your heart, said Ingrid-Simone. —But no, she said, —I believe it is only someone like Clarice who has the nerve to write such awakened shards of hope and despair at once. Is this true? When I nodded, she said, —yes, I've been reading her work. And this gladdened me to such a degree, mostly because she had sought the books out on her own, not quite secretively, but quietly.

—Remember Zerbino? asked Ingrid-Simone. —It's a brilliant passage, isn't it, when she relates her dream about the soft drink that everyone drinks and everyone dislikes but they go on drinking it anyway. It's dehydrating and everyone knows it. They can't stop themselves. Maybe they like feeling thirsty. When I was reading it, even I wanted to try Zerbino, though maybe I've been drinking Zerbino all along.

We talked about Zerbino for a while and then suddenly returned to discussing cream-filled chocolates. Which led to a discussion, quite naturally it seemed, about fortune tellers. We talked about Mr. Rochester telling fortunes in Jane Eyre.

—What a wolf he was, Ingrid-Simone said, —dressed in sheep's clothing, even though it was a red cloak. A many-souled wolf? He tells her she isn't the sort to sell her soul for bliss. He knows her, he understands. And then, it's his own fortune he's telling. And he's interrupted in his interchange with Jane, eventually, by the truth, by an arrival in the form of a visitor, the presence of Mr. Mason. Jane gives him the message of the arrival, it must be her who passes along the message, mustn't it?

How truths are passed from one to another, we spoke about this, Ingrid-Simone and I. Sometimes we pass them, without knowing the message. Secret messages.

And next we spoke about going to a fortune teller ourselves. We were deep in a discussion of how one goes about finding a decent fortune teller when we noticed that Florine was standing near and may have been for some time. We asked her if she might like to come along with us, though honestly, we wanted only to be accompanied by each other.

—I can tell your fortunes, said Florine.

She spoke quietly, in a perfect moment of calm, so that her words seemed to have always hung in the air at that juncture, as though a space had been made for them ahead of their arrival, and that we had always known she was a fortune teller.

—One at a time.

Which reminded me of the Grail Quest, when each of the knights must enter the thick and dark forest alone, at a point where no one else had trod and where the forest was overgrown and difficult to enter. To do otherwise would have been a disgrace.

—One at a time, Florine said, as she ushered me in, as though there were any other choice.

We expected to have our fortunes told together. We expected the fortune teller to have a fancy, made-up name, like Madame Carlota, or Madame Zanzibar, or even Madame Rochester. We both said that to each other afterwards. I was afraid of forgetting what my fortune was, so I wrote it down on post-it notes while Ingrid-Simone was having her fortune told.

Florine led me by the elbow into one of the change rooms with its scent of thousands of ladies raising their arms, a tremendously intimate loaminess, and pulled the velvet curtain around us, tying it with a tasselled rope. A piece of beaded fuchsia silk came from nowhere and she threw it over the plastic chandelier that hung in each fitting salon. I found, in my anticipation to have my fortune told, I could only focus on my inward breath and not the outward one.

I walked into the fitting room, this tiny cramped space, and sat on the overstuffed red velvet chair while Florine sat on a small stool she had brought in. There was no table between us, no crystal ball, no worn cards with pleasantly frightening figures on them or tea leaves to read. Just Florine, sitting, and I, looking at her knees in the warmly worn brown corduroy of her pants. When the curtains were drawn and the cheap chandelier veiled, it was dim and I had the urge to draw my knees up under my chin.

Usually when you go to see a fortune teller, you know the fortune teller is not as she appears. There is an element of disguise: jewellery, scarves, garish lipstick, an overly powdered and rouged cheek. But here, the fortune teller was Florine, the normally secretive Florine. The reverse seemed to have happened. That in taking up the fortune teller persona, she removed her disguise, revealed something about herself, rather than concealing it. We were in the presence of a being who had carefully stepped into herself, so that we were aware immediately that this was her most natural, most comfortable state.

She went into a trance, eyes not quite closed, the way a dog or a baby will sleep and you have to fight the urge to run the palm of your hand over their face to seal them. I kept feeling as though she was about to take my hands in hers, cool and dry, so that I still have the memory of my hands being taken and held. Or were they? I felt myself go into a trance. I don't know how long we sat like that. The air felt like the crackling of Ingrid-Simone's pop rocks, my scalp tingled. I also had this feeling of complete freedom wash over me, which is a ridiculously simple way to describe it. Though this was possibly one of the most extraordinary things I had ever gone through, I didn't write down how I felt at the time though, fearing I might lose it if I did. I'm writing it down now though, in case it's something that Ingrid-Simone also experienced.

I felt suddenly clean, cleansed, purified. Absolved, released. For during the time I spent with Florine, or perhaps Madame Florine or Madame Theodora, I was completely unattached, unconnected from the world and its people. It was like flying, gliding, but maybe the precise word is dreaming, a winged dreaming. And instead of one long pronouncement, there were phrases, sent to me as if in a dream. They were lobbed to me, as a child sends a balloon up into the air with her fingertips.

—There will be a letter. No, two letters. On separate occasions. There will be waiting, there will be beauty in the waiting. This long waiting will be the centre of your life; everything will flower from this, move outward. Your destiny is to be lazy and elegant. Your destiny also is to wait, and to sorrow, responsible, your destiny to worry, and fragments. The letter arrives, a release. But you are not. Released. Found.

And at the word 'released,' I was. At the word 'found', a strange afterthought followed me. I spilled out of the room, without looking back, still in a trance of sorts. I don't remember Ingrid-Simone going in, just a blur off to the side, her entrance, entrancement, a blur.

I should have stood outside, listening. But I was busy scribbling my own lazy and elegant fortune on sky-blue sticky notes and the fleeting thought that it wouldn't be right to eavesdrop passed through me. You see, I did have the thought. Ingrid-Simone came out of the fitting room, through the thick velvet, looking gloriously soaked. At first I was worried, and so was Florine, I could tell. We exchanged a look. But then, she transformed, like Audrey Hepburn at the end of *Breakfast at Tiffany's*, running into the alley in the rain to look for Cat and then Fred, who isn't really Fred, comes. A beautiful, sad happiness. Holly Golightly was drenched in both the sweetest of miseries and the most joyful realization that she was loved and could accept being loved.

I swear the same transformation occurred with Ingrid-Simone the day of our fortunes. Florine watched and said then, in the most normal, every-day Florine voice, —she'll be fine. Which felt like part of Ingrid-Simone's fortune, too. And then Florine disappeared, left the store, though we didn't notice for some time.

I handed Ingrid-Simone my pad of sticky notes, and said, —write. She sat down, with her knees together and toes pointed toward each other. She wrote in her tiny writing, so tiny though this time, that it wasn't legible to me.

When she finished, I tried to tell her about my fortune. Fragments I read to her. I stopped halfway because I don't think she was listening really, which I didn't mind. It seemed wrong to know each other's fortunes anyway, so we both straightened clothes for a time. Ingrid-Simone had a way with arranging the colours just so. When she swept one dress out of the line-up and then put it back a few dresses over, it was a magical thing, the same feeling you get when the last piece of a jigsaw goes into place. Suddenly you saw the design as a whole. The colours of the store radiated, they pulsed, after Ingrid-Simone put them to rights.

It seems odd to me now that we didn't talk more about Florine, how she had revealed herself as a fortune teller. But maybe one more thing just silently clicked into place.

Amsterdam

How to unravel her. A cruel way to describe it, perhaps, but it happened in the smallest increments so it took me ages to notice. That she was unravelling, fraying, becoming undone. Becoming less calm and centred, more frantic. And I was being born into the unravelling.

I'm not ready yet to tell you anything else except ice cream.

She liked to eat ice cream cones. This would not have been quite so remarkable if it had been summer but in the winter it stood out. She made her own at home, constructing them with all the care that a child takes when making a snowman. —It's something I'm quite particular about, she said, —I'm truly beyond exacting about the size of the cone, the weight of the scoop of ice cream. The whitest possible vanilla. It really has to be just so. She liked the cheapest ice cream, the kind that came in big tubs. There's more air in the ice cream and therefore fewer calories.

Some days she arrived at work in the morning with an ice cream cone for breakfast and she hadn't yet taken a single lick. She had that sort of restraint. —The winter is perfect for such a morning meal, she said. —I walked all the way to the work and no melting. And here she twirled the cone slowly, majestically.

—Hmmmmm. Do you know, she said, casually handing me her white-as-snow ice cream cone while she removed her coat and changed into different shoes, —that I never even had an ice cream cone until I was sixteen years old? It was at a friend's birthday party. Well, really she was the neighbour and wouldn't have dared to be my friend, and she was younger than me, fourteen I guess she was. And I was looking over the fence into her backyard, which was barely large enough for a picnic table, oh, quite longingly, and the mother invited me over. Maybe they were surprised that I went. Oh, of course, I'd had ice cream, though not much. We were quite poor, quite poor.

She sat down on the front counter, crossed her legs, and ate the cone in earnest. I turned on the lights and straightened up a little, dusting behind the front counter while she licked her ice cream in a spiral, starting at the top and working her way down. We started swapping, 'we were so poor' stories. I told her about eating cases of canned vegetable soup that had been on sale. The story I wrote down on my sticky note that evening when I went home though was this one: Ingrid-Simone said that after her father left when she was twelve, she was so poor that one day she went to a store and stole underwear. Because she had none. So she took some into a department store change room and put several pairs on and walked out of the store. —I knew it was wrong, but I couldn't go to gym class in junior high without underwear and I didn't know what else to do, she said. —I did make sure that I chose the least expensive and ugliest pairs. She laughed nervously, so that I thought she might cry. And I solemnly agreed, that it seemed like a reasonable act—humiliating but also empowering somehow. That she could take care of herself. Solve problems on her own.

Attached like a burr to my sticky notes about Ingrid-Simone's ice cream cone breakfasts, there was another note I wrote, though it may not have been written on the same day. I don't know when it was written and it doesn't matter, because it was a train of thought that constantly struck me when I was in her presence. The fact of her openness. Words on the light-pink sticky note, such as: giving, refreshing, clarity, open. I never felt as though she was withholding anything. She gave what she could of herself every second, always utterly present. When she laughed it was as though she were placing a gift in your hand. No, it was more than that. It was like being taken to that open space yourself.

But what this set up in me was a kind of ache. A wound of sorts that affected my fragility in unusual ways. I often felt that we were very nearly on the same frequency, our souls, but in truth we were just off from being on the same frequency. And this bouncing back and forth, maybe it was too much.

And now the memory is harrowing because it reminds me that if I had known the right questions to ask, if I had known, things could have been different.

&

I'm racing now to tell you more about her. How long can I hold your attention with my flimsy brushstrokes? I know that she held my attention completely. I went off happily enough to my subterranean job at Theodora's and I endured the women who talked down to us, humiliated us, wore us down with their assumptions about who we were and why we were there, as they tapped the counter when we counted the change back too slowly or rolled their eyes when we couldn't answer their trivial questions. And I put up with the pervasive and at times oppressive scent of the hundreds of homes that had somehow adhered to the clothes, and the dull and mad lowliness of checking pockets for lint and dry-cleaned gum that had some-times even been chewed. And the spot washing of collars and sleeves and crotches and underarms. I endured all these absurd things when I could have been researching a dissertation on women's literature, on the secret marks made in the margins of manuscripts, collecting and comparing notes on the variants of manuscripts, reading between the lines of correspondence and connecting all these with lines from published novels and poems.

Ingrid-Simone and I didn't meet after work. Our entire relationship took place in the cavern of Theodora's in the context of work. But there were several occasions when we met, more or less accidentally, at the Shopper's

Drug Mart on Jasper Avenue, the one that seemed to be a glass palace. She lived several blocks on one side of the avenue and I lived on the other side. In the dark, the store was beautifully lit from the outside and we were moths drawn from our shabby homes into the clean brightness by the obscure and dangerous angles of the glass. Directly we went to the cosmetics. When I first found Ingrid-Simone at the drug store, she was applying eye shadow to her wrist. All the greens she could find so that she had begun to look a little like a space alien. When I pointed this out, she said, —Oh! you're right. I hadn't thought about that. Hmmmmm. Well, you know of course that I am a space alien. I am, indeed.

We always whispered in the sanctum of Shopper's Drug Mart. We were not so much worried about being overheard, but there was something about meeting Ingrid-Simone here, at night, and the way the light shone on us, and the darkness outside, that made whispering seem essential. Anyone walking by might see us in our reverent enchantment, as we wandered from the rows of lipstick and eye shadow to the magazine aisle, where we would silently flip through fashion magazines and *National Geographic* and *Time* and *Oprah.*

We would then maybe saunter down the hair-care aisle, the soap and bubble bath aisle, marvelling at all the scents—lavender, coconut, sage, cocoa, strawberry, vanilla, eucalyptus. We would look at the cold drinks for a surprisingly long time. If we did buy anything, it would be a drink. Something neither of us would usually buy. A Dr. Pepper or a Snapple Peach Iced Tea or a bottle of strawberry milk. We were warm from having stayed too long in the store reading magazines and wandering in our winter coats under the severe and mesmerizing and holy lights. And our thirst, our extreme, unquenchable thirst, always took us by complete surprise.

We would leave, waiting until we were outside to open our drinks. Quietly, we knocked the bottoms of our bottles and popped off the lids, clinking them together. Cheers, we said to ourselves silently, I don't think it was spoken. Swallow and then off in our separate directions. I always looked back after half a block or so but I'm sure Ingrid-Simone didn't. Once, I walked a few steps then turned around and watched her and she never looked back. She was immediately in her own space, you see. I could tell as I watched her walk. She walked as though she were in a dream. A very long and involved dream. I remember thinking I'd give anything to walk into that dream.

One evening, when we were in Shopper's Drug Mart, there was a long line up at the pharmacy counter. We were looking at a display of plum-toned make-up. Lipsticks, eyeshadow and eyeliner. A small television was playing a tutorial on how to create the perfect smoky eyes and we were watching with happily sceptical looks on our faces. Maybe it was our third time through the video. We found that multiple viewings made the experience more pleasantly bizarre. This is when one of the people in the pharmacy line collapsed. We could hear someone calling an ambulance and within a minute we heard sirens. No one moved in to see what was happening. We just stood rooted to where we were.

We watched from our spot in front of the plum make-up display. The line re-formed itself about four feet over from where it had been while the woman who had collapsed remained where she was. Someone draped a white lab coat over her and put a Magic Bag as a pillow under her head. Ingrid-Simone and I watched the line. They continued to look straight ahead. There were a few discrete sidelong glances, over and down and quickly back to straight ahead. Maybe they were being discrete, pretending not to be curious, going about their own business, getting their own prescriptions for whatever pain they might be in, getting their preventatives. Or maybe they really weren't curious. They didn't want to know. Two of the people in the line-up were quietly discussing their places in the queue. One argued that he had been in front of the other in the previous incarnation of the line before it had moved over the four feet. One person strenuously disagreed but the other held his ground, wanting to move up one position. And their whispers became more fierce, until arms were thrown up in the air, and the one in front squared his shoulders and the one behind adopted a stance of vigorous seething, eyes flaming, licking the back of the other's head.

The other customers in the store also went about their business, filling their red plastic baskets with deodorant, conditioner, birthday cards, Band-Aids, antacid, loaves of bread, magazines, rain-scented candles. As the paramedics rushed to the back of the store, I wondered to myself what the other customers were thinking as they casually parted the sea of their consumerism, looking just long enough at what was occurring so that they would be out of the way of the medics. It was not as though any of us could do anything. We all had our own worries, ointments to apply, arguments to resolve, loneliness to abate, orange hair to re-dye.

We stayed at the Shopper's Drug Mart until the lady was taken out on a stretcher and the ambulance drove away, silently. —You'd never know anything happened, said Ingrid-Simone, —it's eerie. And it was. The small crack that the woman had fallen into had closed over. Anyone walking into the store after the ambulance had driven away would have had no inkling of what had just happened. We began to question if it had.

Was anyone else wondering what the fallen woman was going through? The thought had just occurred to me when Ingrid-Simone leaned over and spoke as though she was in a library.

—I wonder, she said, —what she is going through. What falling down in the Shopper's Drug Mart will mean to her life, all of the ripples that will be created from this dropping down. I nodded. I nodded again. She put her chin on my shoulder, lightly, frail.

☙

I arrived at the store the next day and Ingrid-Simone was already there. She was wearing very high heels, ripped and faded jeans, and a floral dress that had once been long. She had raised the hemline and added lace to it. Around her neck was a scarf made from six different kinds of lace she had interwoven with strands of wool and string and bits of fabric.

—It's incredible, I said to her.

—Oh, it's a concoction, she said, —a useless confection. It's ridiculous really, isn't it? But she seemed pleased, pleased with the scarf, she seemed at peace.

There were no customers yet and we went about our business. The store was large enough that we could work in separate corners of the store and feel quite alone, and we were always comfortable with those times. Happy to drift into our own worlds, and later, often we compared reveries.

—Oh, Ingrid-Simone said, —I remembered how last weekend I found a place in the ravine where I could lie down in the snow and no one could see me. I was wearing my long white coat with the white buttons. There was such a gentle slope and I was looking up at the sky, through the tree branches. And I felt like I had disappeared, dissolved, into the deep snow, angelically. It was so delicious, because it started to snow enormous flakes of snow, cotton candy, and I was able to meet them, embrace them and welcome them. I think I slept for a while, so deep was I in the sublime snow, sated, buried. I can't explain it, how tranquil I felt, how loved. Hmm-mmm. I felt like I called down the branches, in my mind's eye, so that I had the most serene daydream of being in a giant nest of my own making, my arms greeting the sky, and all the branches around me. I felt so rested. So embraced. Embraced by the universe, you know?

But maybe this is beside the point. Because while Ingrid-Simone was in the rear part of the store, organizing dresses by colour, and daydreaming and remembering her enchantment in the snow forest, I was behind the counter. I bent to pick up a clump of thread off the floor and put it in the wastebasket nearby. I pulled the basket out from under and noticed a newspaper article had been crumpled and stuffed in and sort of hidden, under another piece of paper. It seemed hidden though maybe it wasn't. I retrieved it, I smoothed. The article was about a woman who had had a premature baby in the Wal-Mart washroom and left it in the toilet. Was the baby alive when it was born? Yes, there were speculations that it had been alive. How could the woman not know she was pregnant even though she claimed this was so? She left it, ran, afraid, and only went to the police station to confess when the story was first reported. There were comments by outraged parents waiting on a list to adopt a baby. There was more wild speculation and the headline "Monstrous Act!" There was an interview with the woman who cleaned the restrooms and had found the baby in the toilet. She was quoted as saying, "I was shocked. I didn't know what it was, how it could be. I thought it must be a doll, someone had bled all over it, you know, the monthlies." And, "It wasn't there the last time I cleaned and then it was there." And, "It made me feel so terrible, so sick. I can't stop having dreams." And, "I'll never be the same inside after what I saw." And, "She's not insane, she's just evil."

Every six months or so there is always a story like this on the news about a woman who didn't know she was pregnant abandoning her baby in a dumpster or on a front step or giving birth in a Wal-Mart or a back alley. Inevitably, there are a requisite number of people who jump on various aspects of the story. There are cries that the mother should be put in jail. The religious people are scandalized, and the barren people who would have taken and loved the child are full of sorrow. Others contend that there's no way you can be pregnant without knowing it, in spite of extensive documentation to the contrary. Comments float that it could only happen to one of those people, whoever those people might be. Racist undertones, questions of how immoral, stupid, poor someone like that must be.

Newspaper articles on these subjects, I noted to myself with sadness, never tried to understand what the woman in question, usually a young woman, was going through, had been through. And then, I stuffed the article back down deep into the garbage and threw the threads on top. For good measure I took a Kleenex from the box we kept behind the counter and threw one of those on top as well.

I tried to glimpse Ingrid-Simone's face but she seemed to be humming to herself, so I took the glass cleaner and went to the front of the store and cleaned the windows and polished the cold doorknobs.

❧

The eye of the hummingbird. From another of Ingrid-Simone's most loved poems, this one by Mary Oliver.

—I was walking down the row of books in the library that must have contained poetry, she said. —I was about to go home, and I was running my hand lazily along the rows as I was going, oh so dreamily. And one of the books leapt out, fell into my hand, so I cradled it. I did, and then it opened to a page, I don't remember opening it you see, which seems implausible, oh, I know that. But it did in fact happen as most implausible things do.

She read:

"Is the soul solid, like iron?
Or is it tender and breakable…

Does it have shape? Like an iceberg?
Like the eye of a hummingbird?"

—Maybe, said Ingrid-Simone, —we are reborn as the eye of a hummingbird, or the bird itself. Free at last to seek nectar, all eye and trembling heart, so alive.

And then there was a very long pause and her heart seemed to me to be trembling, her arms at her side were nearly still but maybe they were vibrating at such a speed that this was invisible. At length, she said, —hmmmmm, a longer than usual hmmmmm. And smiled and shook her head.

⁊

The day we received the fake purse troubled her deeply.

—I just worry that she didn't know, you see, said Ingrid-Simone. —
She, whoever she was, thought she was carrying one thing, and in fact,
it was another. A fake watch is one thing, but a fake handbag—criminal.
The bag is a divine stomach, it contains our most mundane secrets, the
entrails trace how gorgeously ordinary we are. Oh my dear, it's a beauty
factory, a shield, a companion. It's a pretty portable archive, an unconcealed
weapon, a sturdy, personal lost and found. It transforms, transports. It
clutches, snaps, clasps. Thumps and flaps. It spills. You can carry it, lug
it, tote it, schlep it.

She spoke this as if speaking the lines from a Shakespeare play in an
audition, convincing and innocent.

—The purse is a diary containing the scattered sprawl and patient sticky
grunge of life. It's a skin, a husk, it holds guts and gizzards. Think of the
disruptive depths, the darkness of a purse! The purse is a portal, a hinged
door. It's the heavy burden to the bruised portal of our intimate murky
depths, our tranquil and far-off selves. We carry these objects relentlessly,
courageously, anonymously, absentmindedly.

—I cannot help but think of all those fronds and flingings that find
their way into purses. You could reconstruct a life, a woman's life, just by
looking inside, by connecting the dots from one item to the next. A bottle
of scent, a book of poetry, a packet of flower seeds. Pencil stub. Hmm.
Seashell. Feather, of course, a feather. A tin of mints, a telephone book.
Cookie crumbs. A coin from another country.

—Oh, my dear, my love, the quivering lists of things to do, somnolent plots.

—Useful things, things that comfort, things in which to lose oneself. Books.

—One reaches into one's bag. One reaches in and finds. One reaches
into the trembling breath of the bag, the bag breathes in and out, sighs

in silent splendour, sighs with each unclasping, unzipping, unsnapping, unfolding, unflapping. And things, it contains things that endure, that escape me, that are elusive and clamorous and fragmentary.

—A purse may be fancy. It may be slouchy, ornate, cheap, cheeky, flamboyant, chic, humble, durable, bulky, sleek, chunky, iconic, functional, luxurious, formidable, reliable, handy, strappy, smug, witty, thrifty, monumental, classic, coquettish, modest, elegant, discreet, graceful, amusing, clever, coy, natty, extravagant, vital, delicate, glamorous, retro, eccentric, staid. What have I left out?

—In short, a purse is real. It is incontrovertibly real. I won't have that taken away from me, I don't want to be devoured, swallowed by what isn't even real.

❧

I have a particular pile of sticky notes, maybe they are over an inch thick, with a couple of pages from a small notebook sandwiched within. On top of the pile I added one note that said: The Summons. The summons seemed to come from another dimension. Ingrid-Simone and I had been nestling in our separate dimensions together but this was from elsewhere. There had been an early glimmer of spring, the scent of it. After the cold, long winter, the sort of winter that freezes your lungs and contracts your skin and especially your scalp, this moment of spring made us delirious.

When I went home that evening, walking in the unseasonable warmth, the respite, I felt at peace, really at peace. Something I hadn't felt in ages. I felt I was exactly and precisely myself. Clear and fine and unburdened. I felt I was the perfect weight. Not too heavy and not too light and that I was taking place at the proper frequency for my universe.

I arrived home to a blinking light, a message. I noticed how dusty my archaic answering machine was and while I listened to the lengthy message, I massaged the faux wood with a damp cloth.

I had been offered a sessional teaching job at the university, which cata-
pulted me into an immediate state of psychic despondency. As I mulled
over the offer, envisioning myself in a room with students, I began to fray,
revert. There are some intervals when you become acutely aware of who
you are. How at odds with the rest of the world I knew myself to be where
only minutes before I had experienced such peace. How strange, how
weird. I could feel how out of step I was in my skin, my nerves. Does that
seem possible? All those years of trying to 'act normal,' or at least acting as
though I was not constantly terrified, jittery or shattered by academe—I'd
set them aside working at Theodora's. And I didn't want to pretend any
more. But could I work in the basement of a second-hand shop for the
rest of my life? What sort of acting was that?

I always look for what I call little signs. What path to take, what path
to take, I suppose this was my intermittent mantra. Bread crumbs, give me
bread crumbs. I knew to abandon the university because there had been
a culmination of little signs all in one day, beginning with my horoscope
that said: "you will find that you are in the wrong place today but it's not
too late to get to where you need to be." I saved it, folding it up and placing it in one of my three copies of Jane Eyre.

I went out walking later that night amid the streetlights and towering
golden trees, the night of the horoscope, when all the shops were closed,
and I wandered toward the word, Theodora's, which was bright—handwriting that reminded me of my mother's. And the word lodged within
me, so that when I did finally leave the university, when the snow had
fallen and cleansed me and made me long for unsullied sheets of paper,
wordlessness, it seemed proper to walk back toward it.

I escaped. And I knew that I had been right to leave because I didn't
belong, I was in the wrong place. A simple feeling you have as a child at
certain times and know to listen to. And I was very proud of myself for
listening to the feeling.

But here I was being summoned from the extra dimension that we had discovered, Ingrid-Simone and me. We hashed it out for days. The department wanted me to teach a course tentatively called 'literary secrets and genetic criticism,' which was my subject precisely. I was enticed. And then I agreed to teach because how could I not? I agreed before I could change my mind. Maybe my tolerance for being treated like a shopgirl was quite low that day. The tapping of fingers on the front desk when I wasn't moving as quickly as someone wanted, an exchange of looks between friends when I couldn't answer a question about a designer or name the place of origin of a clothing company. The huffing and rude leave-taking of a woman who was annoyed that we didn't have any Chanel dresses in her size and couldn't understand that we were a second-hand store. Maybe that was the day a woman bumped into me while I was doing up buttons on a peacoat. She lurched with her heavily whip-creamed mochacino and spilled a rather generous amount on my sleeve and said nothing. She said nothing even when I let out a little, —oh! She said nothing as I swabbed at it. Nothing. She might have bumped into a post or a tree. I wasn't really there.

Though not yet spring, the birds sang as though it was, and the teaching position at the university wouldn't begin until fall. Agreeing to something so far into the future seemed reasonable enough. But we were both bereft in advance.

ↄ◞

Around the same time, a man I met in a bookstore one evening asked me out on a date. I was lingering. I let my fingers sweep over titles, books in a row; I played the books on the shelf like the end flourish of a piano piece. I listened to the music of the books on a shelf, the hum and hush and vibrations of them. Here is where the cello comes in, and there is where the flute trills, and over here there are kittens purring and the mother cat's deep exhausted breaths.

He was looking down from the top of the stairs on the second floor, holding a coffee, leaning on the bannister. He was at home in the honeyed glow of the bookstore, amid the dark wood and yellow lights. I was in a movie then, I knew I was being watched or knew, anyway, to look up over my shoulder. Embarrassed, I took a book from the shelf and leafed through it, and then, cut, he was standing beside me, telling me that I had chosen well. I suppose these are the sort of scenes that make us believe in the movies, this camera angle and that one, the blinking of the camera that takes us from the top of the stairs to the woman in front of a bookshelf.

I'm a ruthless editor though; I'm leaving a bunch of film on the cutting room floor. Blink, and the camera takes you back to Theodora's, back to the basement, the cavern, the subterranean level where this story takes place. The next day, while Ingrid-Simone polished the scuffs and the residue of dirty pink bubble gum off the bottoms of a pair of black and white pumps, I told her what happened.

—In short, he asked me out on a date, to an opera, to *Rigoletto*. And I've accepted. But now, I tell her, —I'm having second thoughts. Maybe it's too *Pretty Woman*, I said, —okay, without the ride on the private jet. And I don't have anything to wear. Which was true. I had spent the last few years in academe trying to dress invisibly. The clothes I wore at Theodora's, the three outfits I rotated, the grey dress, the black dress, and the long shirt with leggings, were too frivolous for the opera. I had nothing.

—Nothing? said Ingrid-Simone. —Oh, my soul. Nothing? Look, look around you, love.

—Oh, but. I said. And she knew. My electric fear of wearing second-hand clothes was not to be overcome.

She went to the rack with the crimson and cherry and candy-apple red clothes, she knew my size even, and pulled out a killer red dress, swishing it about.

No, my eyes said emphatically, no.

—Okay, then, this. It's black, classic, dressy.

—Just call me Julia Roberts, I said, as she stuffed me into the fortune telling fitting room. That is what we called it, the fortune telling room. We still had the feeling that anything could happen there. When the drapes closed, and they must close dramatically, as is their nature, it was as though you are separated from the world. Or, that you knew you were separated.

I tried not to think about the musty smell of the clothes, the dry-cleaning fluid, the scent of embalming, all the dead people who once wore these dresses, scarves, carried these purses. The distressed and the smug and the broken-hearted and the falsely happy and the preciously simple, all those people for whom these clothes were no longer a fit. Ingrid-Simone threw some jewellery over the top of the drape, next slyly sliding in a purse then a scarf. I heard her walking around the store saying, —hmmmmm. And, —hmmmmm. Clearly enjoying herself.

I didn't want to think about who once wore the dress and on what occasions. So I started to throw out possible topics relating to my situation. I thought about the wardrobe in literature. Symbolism of. The closet. Exits, entrances. The abyss of the swirling dark room. Or was it a womb. The red drape a placenta. I thought about transformations. Eliza Doolittle and *Pretty Woman*. I thought about Cinderella goddammit. About fairy tale fantasy and the expectations and passivity it inscribes in young girls. I thought about waiting, waiting to be saved, and what a ridiculous stance that is but how it made me angry too, because I wanted it, to be saved. I thought about how much I love the scene in *Pretty Woman* when she goes back and tells the saleswoman who had treated her badly that she missed out, using her shopping bags for emphasis. How the movie was a fantasy that never happened to anyone. Not exactly like that. But how beautiful to imagine that it could.

I had the black dress on, and to humour Ingrid-Simone, I draped on the long necklace, I stepped into the shoes. The dress really was quite marvellous, though there was a bit of static electricity until we sprayed it with the big can of static guard. The dress came from what we called the 'fancy racks'—the area where we hung all that glittered, all of the ritzy, high-end, glamorous, big designer-name dresses. It had been dry cleaned but there was still a scent. I had the overwhelming urge to take it off, to get it off of me, it just felt wrong. The wrong thing to have on.

A herd of women came into the store, of course. If I hadn't known better, I would have sworn they all got off the bus at the same time but more likely they all jumped out of their SUVs at the same time. One of them brought clothes in thin plastic shrouds but the rest were on the hunt. We thought they were separate at first, but no, they were all together. They wouldn't say what they were hunting for but they touched everything, taking everything off the racks, creating disorder where we had toiled in a religious manner to arrange our existences. Committing the sacrilege of mixing the reds with the oranges, the lime greens with the forest greens.

—They must all be colour-blind, Ingrid-Simone, scandalized, leaned over and whispered in my ear as I walked by her in my black dress, the shoes clacking with some force as I walked. And then feeling guilty, she said, —oh, hmm, well perhaps some of them really are?

The next hour was taken up with helping our unruly customers find the finery and the accessories to go with their newly chosen pieces, listening to them say crassly, —what a find, what a fiiiiind. Ingrid-Simone sold four purses to three women. When the store cleared, she described the purses to me.

—You know the one with the black beads, gold clasp, the baguette. Hmm. When you opened it, honestly, the scent of French bread, I'm not kidding.

Here, I laughed and asked her to go on.

—Okay. Okay. Hmm. There was the faux fur with leopard spots, the clutch. You would expect the breath of a house cat, but no, when you opened it, roses, the way they smell when you walk into the cooler at the florists, subdued and reserved, but also unimaginably fresh. Then there was the woven leather backpack with the incongruous fringe, yellow and buttery. The scent of erasers and pencil shavings. A bit overwhelming. Lastly. Hmmm. Lastly, a little red velvet satchel. The one I imagined was just like Anna Karenina's, the one she throws onto the tracks before she herself succumbs. The little red bag that delays her, as she struggles to remove it from her arm, oh, why did she not listen to the little red handbag? If only it could have delayed her just another few seconds. Oh, and the exhalation? I had steeled myself for gingerbread, especially cloves, you know, hmmm. But lemon drops, distinctly and irrevocably, lemon drops.

I had a feeling that mulling over Anna Karenina flinging herself under a passing train was not a good place for Ingrid-Simone to dwell, so I distracted her with another outfit change. I had nearly forgotten I was wearing the black dress. I took a brown dress with a white stripe on either side and along the neckline and with a very full skirt off the chi-chi racks. Maybe it was a Chanel or a Chanel knock-off, I had no idea. And I grabbed a pair of low brown pumps, a bit small, but bearable.

—Oh, Shaya, I remember Ingrid-Simone saying. —How beautiful you are! Though I know I am not at all. And then she said, —Shaya, our souls are not aligned for retail are they?

&

Without meaning to, I began writing a paper for a conference I had seen in the department bulletin I was now receiving again electronically since I had agreed to teach the course. The conference was titled, "The Extra-Textual Scribble: Marginalia, Cocktail Napkins, Movie Stubs, and Other Unusual Flotsam of Writers Through the Ages" and would be held in Florence, Italy, in the spring. I sent in a proposal for the paper, on a whim. It seemed a like whim. I said I would write a paper about the use of post-it notes by contemporary writers and ordinary people as well, and compare this usage to past practices. The paper itself, I said, would be written on sticky notes and presented in a power point presentation. I wrote the proposal as an exercise, I told myself. An exercise in writing proposals. And because I had always wanted to see Florence. I honestly had little thought that I might be accepted.

I thought writing notes for my paper on sticky notes, on the notes themselves, made the most sense, and so they ended up in unusual spots around my apartment and even at Theodora's. I wrote about adherence, the minimalism of it. How the inventors had been trying to produce a strongly sticky substance but instead had made a low-level adhesive. Then the question that remained was how to apply the adhesive and so post-it notes were invented. Inadvertently. A mistake had been made and capitalized on.

I liked that the notes don't exact too much, in space and form. They require little, but in their abundance give free rein to the writer. I wrote about how we forget them in certain accumulations, that maybe we are meant to forget. We write on them to remember so that we may forget. I wrote about how they are sometimes difficult to keep track of, especially in instances of overuse. Ingrid-Simone told me that her mother, when signs of her early-onset Alzheimer's began to manifest, used them to remember what things were. On the fridge was a note that said: fridge, the cupboard said: cupboard, and so on.

I also wrote about accretions in writing. About how things build up. About interruptions and interjections and about loss and misplacement. I wrote about the sticky note as a message that could be left in library books, on the doors of bathroom stalls, at bus stops. The post-it as guerrilla art. As a message in a bottle. As fish scales, human fish scales, that we peel from our bodies and place on walls, on desks or kitchen tables. We remove our scales, write on them, and hope they will adhere to certain pages of books—our thoughts sticking to the thoughts of others, or on the fronts of cupboards or fridges. Are they about hope, I asked? And what about a certain type of removal from context? Or sequestering? Words inhabiting a small and circumscribed space. The sticky note as corral. A holding pen.

I talked about how words stick to things, cling, how they flutter off in a strong breeze. How, used too often, affixed too often, post-its lose their ability to adhere. There is a certain angst in thinking about that particularity, in dwelling upon it. I wrote about them as discards, as love letters, as a space to hold meaningless scribbles, offhand thoughts, lists. I wrote about the cultural significance of the to-do list. I wrote about aide-memoirs. I wrote about how they soothed the absentminded, the forgetful, the overwhelmed. I wrote about aide-memoirs as scraps, as slips, as slippages. I wrote about the flesh-toned notes, their affinity with the writer's skin. I talked about sunburn and how the dead white flesh peels away from the body with minimal pain, but that the flesh underneath is suddenly exposed and raw.

My paper was accepted, and instead of being afraid, I was delirious, happy. I felt like I was home. Returning to my people.

∽

I went on the date with the man from the bookstore. And maybe there were sparks, or maybe the knowledge that I was going to Florence in three days made everything seem more romantic, and I was glad that I could seem romantic, knowing otherwise. We agreed to meet again when I arrived back, after my seven days in Florence. I suppose I ought to say more about this date, about Xavier, but when I think of the evening, what I remember most is how after the opera he took my hand and led me through traffic to a café across the street. We wove through cars on the street and I remember noticing the brand names on the hoods of the vehicles. Lexus, Acura, Mercedes, Toyota. How silver they were and how it was not quite dark yet but the lights on the cars shone on each other and the steel shone too. All night I noticed the effects of light.

The stage lighting, illuminating faces, emotions. The colours of the silk dresses, the deep azures, and emeralds, and rubies, imprinted on me in such a way that everything else I saw for twenty-four hours after was seen through a veil of colour and brightness. The light in the café was at first dim with natural light but as it became dark outside, candles were lit on the table. We sat by the window, he in his dark suit, and me in my black dress and low heels, and occasionally I glimpsed our reflection in the dark window and saw two happy strangers, rather aglow. And when we parted we agreed to see each other as soon as I returned and I went to sleep that night thinking about our reflection in the window, Xavier Beauchamp and Shaya Neige. I was attentive to our conversation, enthralled maybe is the proper word, but at the time I seemed to be living in an extrasensory realm that held a meaning I didn't want to ignore either. The way that the candlelight flickered across his hand when he placed it on the table and how it moved with the gestures he made. And how the chandelier, placed high but in the middle of the room, produced a play of light on the floor from its many facets, and that as I stepped on them, I seemed to dance a single dance step as I went by.

When we went outside, the air was cool and everywhere the lights seemed sharp. But also very changeable, fluid. When he walked me to the door of my apartment, the light outside, overhead in the awning, was soft and yellow and we bathed in it for a short while as he held my hand and kissed me and took my key and opened the door for me. When I went inside without him, I felt I must have glowed with that buttery light of a textbook first date. And when I awoke in the morning, the pale light on the wall made me feel that I wasn't quite real anymore, that I had become a little bit of something else, fairylike, maybe, that I had powers involving dust and sparkles. That I could go to the piazza and let birds fly free, whatever the synonym is for that act.

I also felt suspicious, doomed. It was too lovely and that sort of thing only happens in pulp novels. I had glimpsed too many of Ingrid-Simone's romances to believe in the enterprise.

∽

I went to the second-hand shop, to Theodora's, the next two days. Strangely, when I tried to remember the date in any detail, I couldn't. I suspected myself of making it up. Did Ingrid-Simone ask me about the date? She was discrete; she was delighted. It was busy at the store those two days and we couldn't dwell on the subject for any length of time. I was feeling quiet, introspective. And we talked about my trip. In the evenings, I put the final touches on my paper. I practiced my delivery. Read it aloud to a pretend audience. I walked to the Shopper's Drug Mart and bought tiny shampoos and hairspray. When I went to the drug store, I thought I glimpsed Ingrid-Simone, a coat like hers, a stance, a blur, but went about my business, filling my red plastic basket, and when I stood in line, I wondered if she was there and thought I would look for her after I paid, but for some reason, I didn't, I just left. I began to feel stressed, unorganized. I needed to get home and pack and check my documents, print off my paper.

∽

In Italy, it was already spring, already green, that particular new green of spring. I delivered my paper to a small audience and listened to several other papers and drank espresso with colleagues from the United States in cafés, practicing our Italian for a while before lapsing back into English. It was April and there was still snow on the ground when I had left. And when I came back she was gone.

This is what happened according to Florine:

> I came to the front of the store, early in the morning. A woman came
> in with her daughter, who played on the floor in front of the front desk while
> her mother looked around. The child had a purse with her, plastic,
> lilac in colour. And Ingrid-Simone bent down and said —hello, little friend,

what a pretty purse you have. The little girl opened it. I was
waiting to tell Ingrid-Simone something, I don't remember what now.
The purse opened, the plastic handles wrenched by small hands. And
inside was a doll, a naked doll that the child had scribbled on with red
felt pen. So many children do these sorts of things, cut the hair off their
Barbies, you know. But it was red felt pen, indelible. All over the body,
the plastic chubby body.

She stood up. Ingrid-Simone rose. She said, —Yes. She walked out of
the front of the store. I thought she was getting air; she was clearly upset.
I stayed at the counter, expecting. But she didn't come back. And I knew
this was it. This was it for her. I was right because she didn't come in the
next day. I closed the store and walked to her apartment and she let me
in and she was packing. Her mad-money purse, the glitzy sequined thing
in purples and reds and emeralds, sat beside an old brown case, it looked
like a Louie Vuitton case. It might have been, though if it was, she didn't
get it at Theodora's.

I sat on her bed and she packed things into that case, you can't
believe how much she fit into that brown case, it was like a magic trick.
She rolled dresses and shirts into tight cylinders. Shoes went inside shoes.
There was something perfect about the placement of each item. Well, as
she packed she told me that when she was fifteen, I think she said fifteen,
she was at a party at a friend's house and that the world became murky,
wavy, and she didn't remember anything else until the next morning.
She woke up and she hurt though. There was a hurt. —It doesn't matter
who or why, said Ingrid-Simone. —There was more than one. I have a
vague memory of a white bedspread with flowers, very small flowers on
it, the kind that children draw. I never went back and I left school. I
wandered, she said, —I went to the library, I read stories of betrayal, I
hurt. It was a very big hurt, she kept using that word, the h sound was a
long exhalation, and when she said the word it became a wound, a soul-
beating, an abyss.

The word was an abyss. —I was so hurt, she said, —and my body
ached, not just there. She made a motion over her genitals with her hand
open as though it were a hot stove and she'd been burned. —My entire
body hurt, my head hurt, I wanted to sleep and sleep but I wandered. I

remember once I walked down a sidewalk and stopped to lean on each tree on the boulevard for a time, as it was the only way I could make it to the end of the street. My mother was at home in our rented townhouse but she had begun to forget who I was, though neither of us were admitting that yet, and she refused to see doctors and so did I because I was afraid. Without her, I had no one. And I needed her to care for me, to care, even if she didn't always quite know me, even if she had no idea what I was going through. I couldn't tell her.

—I spent hours in the public library and sometimes the university library. I read, but I couldn't think. I wasn't able to think. I absorbed things, stories. They're in me but I'm not sure I remember them. I was remote from myself. I could feel my heart in my chest but I knew it wasn't mine. How could it be mine?

—Some days I would get on a bus and ride to the suburbs, to the Wal-Mart. So far away, Wal-Mart. You could spend hours just walking up and down the aisles and no one would care or notice. I had a route. I walked up one aisle and down the next; I tried not to miss any. First produce and groceries, then the pet food and supplies. Children's toys. Hardware, and sporting goods. Housewares. Clothing. Seasonal. Crafts and sewing supplies. Cards and books. Lamps. DVDs and CDs. Electronics. Games. Printer ink. Tires. Plants. Each time when I was ready to go back to the bus stop I would stop in at the bathroom and someone would have always just cleaned it and signed their name on the plastic-covered sheet that hung on the wall.

—I wandered for five months and maybe it was five months when I was in the loo and the pain was too much so I sat on the toilet and I couldn't get up because my body ached so much. Maybe I was there for an hour or two. It was a meditation. Sitting on the toilet with my underwear around my ankles, holding my dress, twirled in front of me, a long twist. And then a psychic relief. There was a blue light, a huge blue circle in front of me, and then it was around me, straightening my spine. All the pain came at once and then it was gone and I didn't know why but something came out of me.

—Something came out of me, but it wasn't something it was someone. It was someonesomeonesomeone. Which couldn't be. But there was this ugly doll covered in blood in the toilet and I knew it was me. It was me and

I picked it up. I stood up and took my purse off the hook and grabbed the tiny doll with its blood. I opened the stall and found paper towels and wrapped myself, wrapped the doll of me, and put her into my purse, which was a red bag, a doctor's bag. And I took her on the bus, I was on the bus with her and I didn't know I didn't know I didn't know what to do. So I went to the trees that had held me up, I found one of them, alone. We were all alone and I dug a hole in between the roots with my house key and some sticks and my fingernails. I clawed into the earth deep and long and hard and ugly. I did it in the middle of the day and cars went by as I sat on the boulevard, kneeling in the mud, praying into my dress, my soul breaketh my soul breaketh.

—And what do I remember is the dirt, the mud, the way I panted like a dog, panting hard and heavy in the sun, parched and wild, turning into a wild animal, I was baying groaning yelping. I bled from my ache and a little of it went down my leg all the way to my ankle bone. Cars went by, I heard the music pouring out loud into my silence and no one stopped, maybe they thought I was gardening with my red doctor bag, my purse by my side. This girlbabything inside it wrapped in brown paper towels from the Wal-Mart bathroom. I didn't know but I wouldn't even believe that myself. How could I not know? I buried her in the red doctor bag, the red bag was her cradle, her tomb, a womb. I hurt again but it was different, it wasn't my body, it was my soul. It was her soul, I buried her, I buried me, our souls.

ᘒ

And that was all Florine said, all she could say. That's all we knew. Ingrid-Simone never came back to the store.

—Where was she going, I asked. But Florine didn't know. I went the next day to Ingrid-Simone's apartment but there was no answer. The landlord was there and said Ingrid-Simone had turned in her key and I saw that the kitchen chair with crocheted pads for its feet was by the big blue garbage bin in the back alley. She was gone, said Florine, and that's all we knew.

—She did mention the darkness, Florine said. —How the lights surged, the power, and there was a dimness when she sat in the cubicle, in the bathroom stall for so long. How everything had gleamed, the surfaces shone, and everything seemed cheap, cheap metal gleaming. And how in the dimmed room the reflections were dark, and the baby gleamed aglow in the white toilet bowl darkly. I think that's all she said.

She'll be back to pick up her cheque next week, though, I thought, she'll come in and then we'll know. But she didn't come in and Florine put a sign on the door, help wanted. And she hired the first young woman who came in.

The beginning of spring and green was unbearable. I worked with the new person for a while. Her name was Edie, named after Edie Brickell, and she had all of Brickell's songs on her iPod including "What I Am," which was sweet. And she was lovely and smart and capable and tried to make a good first impression. But I was cold to her because I was utterly distraught. And Florine knew I was leaving, going after Ingrid-Simone, and we both knew where.

ↀ

A better writer would end here. The rest would be just life. Which would be more irresponsible? To let you imagine what happened to I.s. in her disappearance, or to imagine it for you. Neither would be true.

I followed her. Or rather, I followed her disappearance. I kept it company; I held the left hand of Ingrid-Simone's disappearance. I did it mostly for myself. I did it because I was terrified. I did it because I needed to listen for her.

> "Put your ear down close to
> your soul
> and listen hard." (Anne Sexton).

I sat on a green bench on the Herengracht in Amsterdam, half a block from the Museum of Bags and Purses. I had been in Amsterdam for a month; I was a fixture. The first week I went into the Museum every day before taking up my stance on the bench. I looked at all the purses and afterwards I waited in the tearoom and looked out the front window. I asked the ladies who served the tea and who worked in the gift shop and who sold the tickets, if they had seen anyone resembling Ingrid-Simone. I found it hard to describe her. —She has dreams pouring out of her, a froth a stream, stars. She's afraid of heights, I said. —You might notice the contractions, I said. —She is giving birth to the spirit of blue hearts like the magnificence of butterfly migration, and she is light-filled and glows like pollen on a white table cloth, she reminds you of threads of saffron on the palm of your lightly stained hand. When you see her you will taste champagne on your tongue, while simultaneously hummingbirds will appear in your mind, and Mozart's music will fill you.

I went to the Museum every few days and the rest of the time I occupied the bench, my laboratory, my workshop. I thought she had been here and she knew I was there too. I thought this because after the first week, there was something scratched into the bench, just where you would rest your right hand if you were sitting in the middle of it, as I usually did. My bag was to the left; I had bought one of the museum's shopping bags that had a photograph of their signature peacock-feather purse on one side and a close-up, a detail really, of the same on the other side. The bag had a zipper so that I didn't have to worry about all my bits and pieces of paper blowing away and was capacious enough to hold the collection of small purses that Ingrid-Simone made for me.

Maybe they had been there all along and I hadn't noticed, two small letters. But you see the sun had come out and I had closed my eyes and put my hand on the bench, gripping it really, because I felt a bit of vertigo, like the bench was a boat and the waters had become a little less calm of a sudden. At first I didn't think anything of the roughness beneath my fingers but something made me lift my hand and look underneath it. The initials, I.s., carved small, ever so small.

Before I left town, before coming to Amsterdam, I went to visit Ingrid-Simone's mother. I knew she lived at an extended care facility called Gardenia Hall. I expected flowers, great vases of flowers in the entryway, on a huge table, and that there would be small vases on the table in the common room where I found Mrs. Stephens. I didn't know her first name but I expected it to be Camellia or Rose or Dahlia or Lily. Anthea, perhaps. I was looking for vestiges of Ingrid-Simone. A bowl of flower petals on a dresser, something she might have left. A small slip of paper with her miniature writing on it, a photograph that, turned over, would have a date on it, names of people.

She didn't speak, Mrs. Stephens, she stared at her hands, and I listened to her breathe in the corner of the common room, alone. The nurse left us before I could ask what Mrs. Stephens' given name was and when I asked Mrs. Stephens, there was only staring and breathing. I listened. I softly told her that Ingrid-Simone had left Theodora's and we were worried. But there was no change in the breathing. There were no flowers in the room. She wore a light blue dress, and the chair was grey and the walls were dove-grey. I listened to her breathe for a very long while, maybe three hours or more, because it seemed a way to pay homage to her existence. And I felt that she was dreaming, though I don't think studies on Alzheimer's patients would bear this out. I expected that she would tell me something extraordinary, which would seem like nonsense but that I could later decode. I thought she might have a moment of violence when I told her about Ingrid-Simone, but maybe she was subdued by drugs or had sunk so far into the abyss of her condition. And though the light in the room was low and filtered, Mrs. Stephens was a shadow, a breathing shadow, wrapped in a white blanket and wearing a most beautiful blue dress, with the most elegant, ankle-length skirt. And her shoes were black, low heels, from the 1950s, a Mary-Jane. The kind that you can dance or take long walks down city streets in. Sturdy, yet elegant.

At one point I leaned in rather close, which may have seemed over-familiar. I thought she was murmuring something, I imagined she said, "my soul breaketh for longing of thee." But I'm sure I only heard this because I wanted to hear it or because it had begun repeating in my head.

There wasn't a single gesture, not when I stood or left the room. I might not have been there. I learned nothing, though I remember the sound of her breathing, soft and even and quiet.

❧

I came to know the purses in the Museum intimately. I stared at them for hours. I spent a lot of time wondering who made the beaded and hand-worked bags from the 18th century.

I loved looking at the embroidered bags, the reticules and the silk letter cases. One of my favourites was a deep red velvet satchel dating from the 17th century. At the end of the drawstrings were three ornate silver balls and a silver key and I imagined the key had magical properties, that it might open up other realms and that one day I would write a book about that purse, that key. After gazing at the velvet purse, I headed to the Chatelaines. I thought Ingrid-Simone would like these, the small objects hanging on chains. There were miniature scissors, pincushions, thimbles, knives, fans, perfume bottles, dance cards, and even a miniature purse made of silver mesh.

Walking through the museum, I tried to hear the breathing of the purses, as Ingrid-Simone would. And I thought I did hear them, in the Lucite purses, in the flapper bags from the 1920s, in the Kelly bag, and in the bags shaped like telephones or champagne buckets or adorned with images of flamingos or Madonnas. When I left the museum to take up my life on the green bench, I was drained. Even though the handbags were all behind glass, I felt like I had been breathing in the lives of all the women who had once owned these bags.

Sometimes I watched the short film on the history of the museum or glimpsed it as others watched it. I loved the part where the opening of the museum is filmed and all the women are walking around with their own purses, looking at the purses. When I sat on the bench, I had a heightened awareness of all the women carrying bags and purses and the film continued in my mind. Women glided by on their bicycles on their way to work with medium grey satchels across their bodies. Tourists walked by gripping their handbags. And I sat on my bench, with my huge shopper and my smaller handbag, and none of us knew what the others were carrying. I pulled out my book on the bags in the museum and looked up the plastic, see-through ones on page 278 and 279. But even these didn't offer up perfect clarity— one was adorned with pink fabric flowers and the other was faceted in the manner of cut crystal. To every disclosure there is a degree of obscurity, at times a softening, a veil of flowers.

ↄ⁄ↄ

There were a few books in my peacock-feather bag. In one I read, "It's never quite right to make a character disappear or die." And I moved from that passage and read the line from Clarice Lispector that "each of us is responsible for the entire world." I was dedicated to being the instrument of Ingrid-Simone's reappearance. I was dedicated to listening for her footsteps over my right shoulder. Waiting. Keeping her disappearance company.

ↄ⁄ↄ

One afternoon, I sat on the green bench on the canal and wrote for hours, all the thoughts that came into my head. An entire notebook of stream-of-conscious thought, of wandering. And while I did this, I listened for her,

I felt as though I would know if she were coming toward me, over my shoulder. That I would feel the disruption the air would make.

I wrote down her favourite lines from Rumi, "What is the soul? / I cannot stop asking. / If I could taste one sip of an answer, / I could break out of this prison for drunks." Had she tasted one sip of the answer?

I wrote down things I noticed when we worked together that winter at Theodora's. I had noticed that when she spoke to a woman who came into the store, or maybe two friends, that she would often be ignored. It was a strange phenomenon so far as I was concerned. They would ask her something and she would respond, intelligently and to the point. But the two friends would suddenly talk over her, cut her off, forget that she was there, looking right through her with glazed eyes. Ingrid-Simone would be left standing mid-sentence with her mouth open. Once, she glanced over at me and pulled a face, rolled her eyes and stuck out her tongue. The women didn't even notice. She mouthed to me, see? Then she shrugged and walked away, looking at me over her shoulder with a smile. Later, when we talked about what had happened, laughing at the complete rudeness of these two women, she said, —Oh, Shaya, this happens to me all the time, love, all the time.

—It's because you're on a different frequency, I said fervently, —a more mystical frequency. You have a dimension too many, I said, quoting from Steppenwolf.

—That's lovely, Shaya, hmmmmm, she said, and paused a rather long time. —But I understand that they see I'm nothing. Which is interesting in a way, isn't it? How little I register, how small it is possible to be. How insignificant. How inconsequential. And then, I do think that some people must feel that to rob a small creature's dignity from them gives them more power. Do you think, Shaya?

I don't remember what else we said to each other after that. But I remember how I felt near the end of the winter, how these daily slights compounded, how they wore us down and made us soul-heavy, so that we couldn't laugh as much anymore about them. How we became frayed and maybe dangerous because of them. We were bored, had exhausted the possibilities of the store perhaps. We became less of ourselves. And tired, how tired we became. Always yawning. I remember Ingrid-Simone once put her head on the front desk late one afternoon, how she fell asleep, standing. I thought she was joking. I'm not sure how long she stayed like that but the front door opened and the bell jangled and she sang out so beautifully, — hello, welcome to Theodora's, which is something we had long given up on doing. Even when we walked right up to customers or stood beside them and said hello, how many times did they not return the hello? No time for hello. We were of no consequence and didn't deserve the courtesy. Instead, they launched into what they had come for, their wants. We still greeted people who were in our vicinity or those who approached us but we had certainly given up saying hello to anyone who walked into the store.

I remember Ingrid-Simone wincing once, shuddering, when I likened us to Wal-Mart greeters. For a split second, I think she doubled over, I imagine she had, as if she'd been punched in the abdomen, feeling a deep psychic pain. But then she raised an eyebrow and said, —oh no love, I'm sure they get paid far more than we do.

I remember nodding and saying to Ingrid-Simone, —hmmmmm.

And she responded, —hmmmmm.

Then we went back to whatever tedious task we were doing.

⌘

She was the sort of person who crossed the street without looking over her shoulder.

She was attuned to birds flying overhead, could feel their shadows before she saw them. She loved when this happened and followed the shadow with her eyes as long as she could. Had often broke into a run without realizing it for several paces, trying to catch up to the shadow of a crow or a seagull, her hand outstretched.

She too loved the book Jane Eyre and could feelingly recite many lines from the book. When Jane says to Rochester, "Do you think because I am poor, obscure, plain, and little, I am soulless and heartless? You think wrong! —I have as much soul as you, —and full as much heart! And if God had gifted me with some beauty, and much wealth, I should have made it as hard for you to leave me, as it is now for me to leave you."

She made me a purse dedicated to Charlotte Brontë, in moss green. Inside were the items Jane Eyre took when she left Rochester and Thornfield Hall. Some linen, a locket, a ring, a smaller purse containing twenty shillings. The handkerchief and the gloves that she attempted to trade for a bread roll.

❧

She noticed how women carry their handbags and divined meaning from it. Over the shoulder, across the body, under the arm, dangling from the arm, gripped. —I once saw a woman who would find a wall to put between her hip and the purse, she said. —I followed her around the mall one day when I was there. She would stop to look at something and take it to the nearest wall, where she would place her purse and then throw out her hip to meet it almost like the beginning of a dance. She stopped to buy a coffee and then stood to drink it for a while, with her purse against the wall. I've seen women who trailed their purses from one finger. Some prefer the wrist. I've seen women put their purses between their legs, or hold them in their teeth. I've seen them tangle the strap of their purses around their arms or hang them so low they nearly reached their knees.

—You can tell so much about what a woman is going through by the way she holds her purse. Is she composed and serene? Or has she lost her nerve, hanging on by a thread…

☙

She seemed happiest when cleaning the purses, repairing them. She used Crazy Glue to affix loose rhinestones. She had a special cloth to shine leather and another cloth for the insides of the purses. Sometimes I saw her open a purse and say into it, —hmmmmm, almost as though she were trying to resuscitate it. Maybe she was saying hymn, a prayer. When I caught her eye after she has did this, she laughed so infectiously.

☙

I wanted to write about her as beautifully and as tenderly as love. I wanted to say that I sat on the green bench and meditated solely on Ingrid-Simone. I had an idea, that if I could concentrate perfectly on her, focus my attention with devotion and clarity, that she would reappear, return. And if I spent time learning about purses and handbags and frequented her yearned-for Museum of Bags and Purses, that would be my way of keeping her company.

I made lists of all the names for handbags. Clutch, reticule, pouch, pocketbook, balantine, sac, duffle, rucksack, messenger, grip, workbag, evening bag, dance bag, saddle bag, Kelly bag, carpetbag, backpack, chatelaine, minaudiere, baquette, hobo, satchel, petite portmanteau, bracelet bag, lunchbag, boudoir bag, miser bag. This list became a mantra for me and I repeated it as I walked back to the small flat I was renting. My favourites were, reticule, clutch, and portmanteau, as this combination made for a nice walking pace, I found.

☙

She had made me one last miniature purse, though at the time I didn't know it was the last. But first there was a large white handbag, in honour of Clarice Lispector. Full of flowers. Ingrid-Simone had watched the YouTube video of the only time Clarice Lispector was ever interviewed on film, near the end of her life. She sat in an awkward leather chair in a desert of a studio. She held a large white purse in one pale hand and a cigarette with the other. Not understanding Portuguese, Ingrid-Simone listened to the spaces and silences and pauses. —Her pauses, said Ingrid-Simone, —were the most insightful and holy pauses I have ever heard.

She had read *The Stream of Life*, the book that I most revere, the book that is for me, even in translation, the book beyond all books. It made me feel as though we are part of a flow; that life continues, that life goes on, as they say. As someone who embraced the study of genetic criticism, I was fascinated to read about Clarice Lispector's friend Olga Borelli— how she had helped her structure the book. "Delicate interventions" they are called in the biography of Clarice Lispector, *Why This World*. Olga is quoted as describing the process of editing the book as "breathing together, it's breathing together."

I read this book, this biography of C.L., when I worked at Theodora's with Ingrid-Simone. I even wrote the author, Benjamin Moser, a short message on Facebook and he wrote a short note back, which made me happy. An acknowledgement of an acknowledgement. I remember thinking that when I read the line about breathing together my process and obsession with being the secret chronicler of Ingrid-Simone's life was described. All the strange bits of paper I wrote on when I got home from work, sitting in my chair covered with the rough turquoise fabric. Even in the store I wrote on scraps. I became less and less secretive. Sometimes I wrote on the back of a receipt that someone didn't take. I wrote down things while Ingrid-Simone spoke and her eyes twinkled. Did she think I was writing down a poem, or a note to remind myself to purchase milk on the way home? I don't think so. I think she knew more or less what I was up to. That I was attempting to take her likeness, as an artist would, to draw the contours of her face, her jet-black hair, her lovely olive skin. But I was doing this with scant words, scrawls and word impressions. At times I tried to write quickly enough to document exactly what she said but I was never quick enough. I wanted, if nothing else, to capture the particular way she breathed, her pauses. The way the short film of Clarice Lispector captured Clarice's breathing, her smoking, the way she was burned on one hand, and the way she clutched her large pure white and holy handbag.

I recounted the recollection of Olga Borelli to Ingrid-Simone —where she talks about her friend, how she kept the fragments of *The Stream of Life*, some of which were written on "the back of a check, a piece of paper, a napkin." Borelli went on to say, "I still have some of those things at home, and some of them still even smell of her lipstick. She would wipe her lips and then stick it in her purse."

The miniature purse that Ingrid-Simone made to honour Clarice Lispector was white, larger than the other purses she had made, but still tiny. Within: a tiny typewriter, a piece of paper with words and lipstick, a turtle, and flowers. A rose, a violet, a sunflower, a daisy, an orchid, a tulip. One of everything you might conjure in your mind when you think of Clarice Lispector. The purse was overrun with flowers. The sadness of flowers.

The last purse was one for me, Shaya Neige, full of snow and sticky notes. "Remember me", one yellow scrap said. How could I not? The tiny purses, like gondolas, skimming toward me, down pre-ordained canals, untraceable.

❧

I walked over to the Albert Cuyp market and wandered through the throngs of people, so many tourists. I bought frites and mayonnaise, rather than my usual tomato soup from the restaurant on the opposite corner, then hurried back to my bench. I was always worried that someone else might take it up but this never seemed to be the case. Once in a while someone alighted in my absence but they didn't stay long. Perhaps they sensed me hovering, they sensed my need.

I slowly ate my frites and though I tried to concentrate on Ingrid-Simone, my thoughts moved from her to the store, to Florine. I said I would keep in touch with her but I saw no point and as yet I haven't. I thought back to the day in the hayfield, how hot it was, the intoxicating smell of new-mown hay. I remembered the bicycle, the familiar feeling I had when the woman named Maureen on the bicycle spoke. Her plaid shirt. I remembered wiping the sweat from my brow, how heavy my bag felt. All the thoughts I was trying to walk out of my head. The way a very long walk can empty you, still those voices that disrupt, that worm and stammer into you, that are stronger and more persistent than breath. And it occurred to me that this woman on the bicycle, maybe she was not Florine at all.

The more I thought about the woman on the bicycle and Florine at Theodora's in the back room or Florine the Fortune Teller—Madame Theodora, the further apart they seemed. I could no longer remember why I thought one was the other, though their names did rhyme. Maureen, Florine.

☙

On one of the earliest slips of paper, I had written: It's not so much that she's innocent, it's that she's very open, an exposed nerve. Maybe her entire nervous system is exposed. I think now that Ingrid-Simone was able to walk through the world in this way because she was also enthralled. Her sorrow, her wound, was so exposed that she seemed more real than ordinary people, more real than you or I. Her sorrow had transformed her so that she had the radiance of divinity. You might think this can't happen in our century but it can. Usually when I picture her in my mind, she becomes something beautifully and intimately remote, serene and light-filled, like a young woman in a Vermeer painting. But sometimes she resembles the rough painting of Rouault's king. Thick black outlines, jewel-toned panels.

The layers and layers of paint, the way that a glimmer of one colour is revealed below by the swipe of a brush over top, spreading another colour, concealing. In the Rouault paintings, I marvelled at the layers of sorrow, covered and covered, one bound to another as a salve. Built up until every sorrow is hit upon, every possible kind. And in Vermeer's paintings, it is thinned. Painted so slowly. Light forms like honey in every recess, every opening, until everything is open and everything is secret. The paint encompasses everything around sorrow, the serenity, everything but sorrow, so that you can't help but feel how stunning sorrow is as well.

∾

The thing I have refrained from mentioning is Ingrid-Simone's purse. How she never carried one herself, and how I never noticed that until I was sitting on the bench.

∾

The bench. My green boat, my perch, my private waiting room.

At first I was patient, expectant; I waited with a purpose. She would arrive. I thought frequently of the Grail King myth at the point where Percival enters the story. He has his moment, he might ask the question, he might be splendid, spontaneous. But the question is entangled in his ideas of propriety, of all those things he has been conditioned to believe. He is in the same room as suffering, but cannot ask. Time is fleeting, he doesn't have long to speak the question. He must be spontaneous. His chance. It passes by.

"The key to the Grail is compassion, suffering with, feeling another's sorrow as if it were your own. The one who finds the dynamo of compassion is the one who's found the Grail." This is what Joseph Campbell says. The Grail isn't an object; it's a state of being. Percival failed in the Grail Castle. I failed in *Theodora's Fine Consignment Clothing*.

I sat on the green bench, gripping it; the bench gripped me. I might have been buried in a mound of soil, my bag beside me. I overdid the bag, visited the museum, read through the catalogue I bought. I ran an inventory through my head of all the bags that Ingrid-Simone had cleaned and repaired and loved and hated at Theodora's. And then I thought of all the little bags inside my bag, the ones she made for me. Literary handbags.

☙

I rehearsed what I might say to her or ask her when she appeared, when she moved my bag over and sat beside me on the bench.

At times, I wrote notes on the green bench. I transcribed what I jotted down on the scraps and bits of paper, on the ticket stub from the Jane Eyre movie I went to see at the Princess Theatre. At times, I felt lazy. I felt the futility of the procedure. What did I hope to accomplish by remembering someone in this way? Maybe it was akin to seeing faces on milk cartons. There was a slim chance that someone might recognize a child or themselves as a child. To be found. Or, if not that, the viewer might once again realize the tenuousness of things, to cleave to those they hold dear.

I thought of her as my accomplice. At times, I felt so horribly alone. The purpose for the notes had changed. The notes were no longer for her; they were for me. Maybe they always were. Of course.

☙

I reached a point where I realized I didn't need to remember or know everything about her. Didn't need to write anything else down, to elaborate, to repeat things. I needed to sit and wait. Devotedly. Single-mindedly. I needed to keep her disappearance company, only that. Such an intimacy, this solitude, a juicy grandeur, an acquiescence to her essence.

cro

I took notes from the moment I met Ingrid-Simone. A compulsion that became a habit, recording her, her existence, on insubstantial slips of paper. I often wrote descriptions of her outfits. Sitting on the bench gave me an opportunity to sort the notes, so I could assemble all the ones on her outfits into one stack.

—powder blue fortrel suit, flared pants, large lapels, hand sewn in the mid 1960s, large white floppy brimmed hat (straw), white ankle-length vinyl boots
—floor-length hippy dress, Empire waist, flounced sleeves, wooden bangles, wooden wedges, real daisies woven into a crown
—business suit, men's wear inspired, but with extremely feminine touches, pink high heels, pink Lucite necklace, cotton candy pink nail polish

I took notes at first because I wanted to understand her. I knew she was someone beautiful, unconventionally beautiful. She herself was interested in what was considered to be so, aesthetically. What was pleasing, what could be brought into the realm of the fashionable. She had made it a quest to rehabilitate discarded things by re-contextualizing them. She looked at a blouse on the metal hanger rack and we exclaimed at how perfectly hideous it was, how no one sane would buy such a thing. But in the next breath, she said, —hmmmmm, well, well. Let's try looking at this another way then. What if we un-tucked this belt, cut the flouncy scarf off. Oh no, worry not, my Shaya, no one will notice. Then let's pair it with these jeans and this black netted scarf. And honestly, you wouldn't have guessed it was the same blouse at all.

I wondered how souls intermingle, if her soul had in some way become part of mine. I thought about proximities, how they affected us. How we spent so many days together, eight hours a day, Tuesday to Saturday. Characters shouldn't disappear in novels but in real life we disappear from each other all the time.

I thought a lot about the contrast between the bathroom stalls at Wal-Mart and the ones at the Museum. I wondered if Ingrid-Simone had been to the café at the museum and if she had ordered a little purse-shaped bon-bon to go with her coffee. I wondered if she went to the loo and if the beautifully lit silvery purses in the glassed-in niches found in each stall made her happy. I thought they would. Or they may have made her cry and cry. I know I wept when I first saw them, but that after, they only made me smile.

The end of the summer. I began to look wild in the eyes, unkempt, besieged by emptiness, by no one. Weary. Plainer than usual. Hair tied back, same clothes in rotation. I remembered reading Deleuze on Beckett, how he said that we should "distinguish between Beckett's 'lying down' work and his 'seated' work, which alone is final. This is because there is a difference in nature between 'seated' exhaustion and the tiredness that 'lies down,' 'crawls,' or 'gets stuck.'" And how I wanted to lie down on the bench some afternoons, early evenings. But when this feeling overtook me, instead, Jane Eyre-like, I called things out over the canal.

Are we not ensouled? Are we not entwined? Have we not made a mark on each other, however slippery the soul might be? We do care for each other, we do! And so on.

There was no response. No feeling that my words had met another soul, nor Ingrid-Simone's.

⁊

What day did I abandon my bench and wander into the Rijksmuseum? I waited in the line-up for a couple of hours. I was drawn to *The Kitchen Maid*. Vermeer. The light coming in through the window that rests so humbly on the maid's hands and on the golden front of her dress and on the milk pouring into the bowl. The painting is made of honey rather than paint and canvas; it is made of light. She, the painting, is a reminder that all of us are immortal, none of us are ordinary, could we be merely ordinary when the light that we may find ourselves bathed in is the portal to all our innocent secrets? That the light itself is the secret, the way it can hold us, and hold others, those who might be arrested by such an acute glimpse into portals, where the connection of souls may be witnessed. Van Gogh once wondered, how to get inside a star? We are there, standing by a window, doing chores, light easing in, but a light that is interior, the light of the soul, glowing and glowing.

A couple of nights before I left, I had a dream. In the dream I opened my peacock shopping bag and I took out the miniature purses that Ingrid-Simone made for me. I dropped them down into the canal one by one as a swan skimmed by, surrounded by the purse boats. When they were out of sight, I upended the rest, all the contents of my bag, all the leaves of paper and post-it notes, the paper napkins, the chocolate-bar wrappers and the small blue reporter notebooks I had filled with notes and thoughts on Ingrid-Simone and the ones inspired by her.

I returned to teaching in the fall, to take up my PhD again. My heart was mostly in it, though not completely. But perhaps this has made me a better teacher, a better student, because I was better at discerning where and how others were having difficulties with the material, how they could bring more of themselves into it to make the work meaningful. I took the line by Goethe to heart: "If I accept you as you are, I will make you worse; however if I treat you as though you are what you are capable of becoming, I help you become that." This made all the difference for me. Whereas before I was consumed by my own fear, now I concentrated on the becoming, the birthings, the progress and process of souls, the wolf-light that emanated from each being.

How easily distracted I was that summer in Amsterdam after the winter of I.s. Maybe I stayed on the bench because it was the only place I could hope to keep my mind on her. And what if she had come walking up from behind? Or if I had seen her from my perch in front of the Museum of Bags and Purses? Or if I had been sitting in the café in the Museum eating a bon-bon and she had sat at the table with me? Or come upon me when I was looking at the purses for sale in the gift shop? How would I have behaved and what would she have said? I realize that I would have still forgotten or refrained from asking the question. Being there on the bench was not the same as asking the question.

It's difficult to hold someone like Ingrid-Simone in one's mind for any length of time. I already doubt that I knew her.

And even though it was a dream, I decided the next morning, before breakfast, to enact it. I sensed this was something Ingrid-Simone would approve of. I set sail to her purses, to all my notes, maybe even to my dream. Like in the story of Rumi's father's notebook. Rumi's luminous friend, Shams, interrupts a conversation between Rumi and his students. They're sitting on the edge of a fountain, and Shams pushes the notebook into the water. "It is time for you to live what you have been reading and talking about. But if you want, we can retrieve the book. It will be perfectly dry. See? Dry."

My notes were not so easily retrievable, nor did I, at the time, wish for them to be so. And I haven't regretted letting them go. But even so, the summer after my first year back in academe, I reconstructed my notes from memory. I tried to be as faithful to my somewhat illegible scribbles, my fragments, as possible. I sat on my balcony that summer with another notebook, a very thick one, with green lines. I wrote down everything I could remember, everything I had scribbled on so many scraps of paper. And then I transferred it to my computer the following summer, so that by now several years have passed.

I have also painstakingly documented the process of my compulsion, my reconstruction of these scratchings, starting from when I set my notes loose into the Herengracht canal. It began: today I set sail to my winter notes, my I.s. notes, and worse, I sent Ingrid-Simone's small purses into the thick and impenetrable water because I thought they'd be safest there, heading to the sea, embracing the depths. I'm both proud of this act and ashamed. I heeded my dream and heedlessly spilled them into the immense and incomprehensible stream of life because I knew I couldn't carry them, they couldn't be held or carried or contained.

I wrote about reconstructing my notes in the summer when I was writing about winter. How I had to take an ice cube out of the freezer some days and hold it in my left hand while writing with the other. I felt the cold melting through my fingers and down my bare leg. Sometimes I held a cube of ice on the back of my neck and felt the cold water skating down my spine. I wrote about how the bits of paper floating down the stream would come to me in dreams, how I would see them floating away. They became part of another unconnected dream but when I woke up all I could remember were these scraps floating away from me, by me, through my fingers.

I wrote about how I conjured these lost notes. Instead of trying to reconstruct them chronologically, I attempted to remember them in categories. First I tried to conjure all the marginalia —the notes that I wrote in the margins of the notebooks or things that I added to a note jotted down on a napkin or a movie stub. Then I worked on remembering the notes I wrote in restaurants, on napkins usually. Then the notes that were on ephemera and in this category I included bill stubs, movie stubs, lottery tickets. Next came the post-it notes. Sometimes I could remember what colour the note was on that I wrote a particular observation. Then came the notebooks, first the reporter style notebooks, and then the slightly larger ones.

I wrote about the space that followed, where I wrote nothing. I wrote about lacunas, those gaps in writing indicated by brackets and ellipses. I filled up pages and pages with them because it seemed the most honest thing to do.

[…]

[…]

I wrote notes about light. All of those occasions where the light seemed to emanate from beyond. I wrote notes about the soul and sometimes these two categories overlapped. The soul is light. I.s. is light. I wrote down the words, soul, I.s., light.

Sometimes I wrote about those things that I knew I couldn't quite remember. There was a glimmer of a memory but I couldn't quite remember how it had gone. I wrote about how even though I could remember many of the things I notated, I knew that I worded everything differently in my reconstructions. I imagine it was not dissimilar to the process that translators go through, though in my case I was translating memories as faithfully as I could. I wanted to keep the authenticity of the original, but was hampered by my own poor memory.

And this—all my thoughts on the process of translating air and love and the dark and unknowable recesses of handbags—has ended up being my dissertation, soon to be published by a prestigious university press. Which I suppose seems odd, that the book beside the book of I.s. would be published.

But I want to leave a copy of this, a reconstruction of the floating fragments and purses and birthings and Ingrid-Simone, the biography of a young woman one winter, the book I couldn't write and did write, the subject of my dissertation you could say, on the green bench near the Museum of Bags and Purses. I'll have it bound, a single copy, and take such pains on the cover of the book. I want it to be eye-catching, something that Ingrid-Simone would notice and be delighted by. I want her to know that I understood something of what she was capable of becoming, and is.

Acknowledgements

In February of 2011, I convinced my husband Rob, and daughter Chloe, to travel with me to Amsterdam to visit among other museums, the Museum of Bags and Purses which had begun to figure in the book I was writing. I'm grateful to them for journeying with me with such interest and delight, both to Amsterdam, and in life. This book is for them.

I thank my friends in writing, in particular those who read this in an earlier form. Kimmy Beach, Nina Berkhout, Lee Elliott, Barb Langhorst and Annette Schouten Woudstra. Thank you to Dawn Kresan for a splendid cover. Thank you to Aimee Parent Dunn for being the perfect editor for this book.

Author Biography

Shawna Lemay is a writer, blogger, photographer, and library assistant. She has written six books of poetry, *All the God-Sized Fruit*, *Against Paradise*, *Still*, *Blue Feast*, *Red Velvet Forest*, and *Asking*, as well as a book of essays, *Calm Things*, and an experimental work, *Hive: A Forgery*. Her first book won the Stephan G. Stephansson Award and the Gerald Lampert Memorial Award. She lives in Edmonton.